SPOOKSVILLE

3-Books-in-1!

D0109527

Don't miss the rest of the Spooksville series!

SPOOKSVILLE

3-Books-in-1!

The Secret Path
The Howling Ghost
The Haunted Cave

Christopher Pike

Aladdin
NEW YORK LONDON TORONTO SYDNEY NEW DELHI

ALADDIN

An imprint of Simon & Schuster Children's Publishing Division
1230 Avenue of the Americas, New York, New York 10020
This Aladdin paperback edition September 2015
The Secret Path text copyright © 1995 by Christopher Pike
The Howling Ghost text copyright © 1995 by Christopher Pike
The Haunted Cave text copyright © 1995 by Christopher Pike
Cover illustration copyright © 2014 by Vivienne To
All rights reserved, including the right of reproduction in whole or in part in any form.
ALADDIN is a trademark of Simon & Schuster, Inc.,
and related logo is a registered trademark of Simon & Schuster, Inc.
For information about special discounts for bulk purchases, please contact
Simon & Schuster Special Sales at 1-866-506-1949 or business@simonandschuster.com.
The Simon & Schuster Speakers Bureau can bring authors to your live event.
For more information or to book an event contact the Simon & Schuster Speakers Bureau
at 1-866-248-3049 or visit our website at www.simonspeakers.com.
Series designed by Jessica Handelman
Cover designed by Neil Swaab
Interior designed by Mike Rosamilia
The text of this book was set in Weiss Std.
Manufactured in the United States of America 0222 OFF
4 6 8 10 9 7 5 3
Library of Congress Control Number 2015939877
ISBN 978-1-4814-5745-3 (pbk)
ISBN 978-1-4814-1051-9 (*The Secret Path* eBook)
ISBN 978-1-4814-1054-0 (*The Howling Ghost* eBook)
ISBN 978-1-4814-1057-1 (*The Haunted Cave* eBook)
These titles were previously published individually by Aladdin.

Contents

THE SECRET PATH

For Pat, my editor

1

For Adam Freeman, moving to Spooksville wasn't something he'd planned. But being only twelve, he hadn't a lot to say in the matter. They had to move, his parents said, because of his father's job. Of course, when they told him about Spooksville, they didn't call it that. Springville was the proper name of the small oceanside town. It was only the local kids who called it by the scarier, but more accurate, title. It was only kids who knew how weird the place could get after dark.

Or even during the day.

That was the thing about Spooksville.

Not all its monsters waited until the sun went down to appear.

Unpacking the moving van and carrying his stuff up to his new room, Adam wasn't thinking of monsters or the supernatural. But that was soon to change. Oh, yes, in a big way.

"Adam," his father called from inside the truck. "Can you give me a hand with this love seat?"

"Sure," Adam replied, setting down the box of clothes he was carrying. He enjoyed helping, even though his muscles were still sore from loading the truck two days ago in Kansas City, Missouri. His father, who was something of a nerd, had driven straight through to the West Coast town. Adam had slept on a rubber mat in the back of the truck. The road had been rough.

Adam was small for his age, but he was growing steadily and figured he'd catch up soon. The problem was he had no one in particular to catch up to now that all his friends were over a thousand miles away. Adam thought of Sammy and Mike as he climbed into the truck. He wondered what they were doing right now. His father paused to stare at him.

"What's that look?" his dad asked. "Are you homesick already?"

Adam shrugged. "I'm okay."

His dad ruffled his hair. "Don't worry. You'll make new friends soon. Not all the cool guys live in the Midwest." He smiled as he added, "Not all the cool girls live there either."

Adam frowned as he leaned over to pick up his end of the short sofa. "I'm not interested in girls. And they're definitely not interested in me."

"It's when you're not interested in them that they start to chase you."

"Is that true?"

"Some of the time, if you're lucky." His father leaned over and picked up his end. "Let's lift on the count of three. One—two—"

"Why is it called a love seat?" Adam asked. He was curious about many things, even things he pretended to have no interest in.

"Because it's only big enough to fit two lovers. Are you ready? One—two—"

"You know I didn't really know any girls in Kansas City," Adam added hastily.

His father stood up again and stretched. "What about Denise? You saw her all the time."

Adam felt his cheeks redden. "Yes. But she was just a friend. She wasn't a . . ." He struggled to find the right word. "She wasn't a *girl* girl."

"Thank God for that." His father leaned over again. "Let's just lift this thing and get it over with. One—two—"

"Three!" Adam said as he yanked up hard, catching his father by surprise.

"Ahh!" his father exclaimed, and dropped his end. He clutched his lower back and his face twisted with pain.

"Did you hurt yourself?" Adam asked, thinking what a stupid question it was. His father waved him away as he limped down the ramp of the truck.

"I'm all right. Don't worry. Just a pulled muscle. We need a break anyway."

"I'm sorry."

"It wasn't your fault."

Adam was concerned. "Are you sure you're all right?" His father wasn't exactly in perfect shape. In the last couple of years he had grown a fair-size belly. Too many doughnuts and sodas, Adam thought, even though those were two of his favorite foods too. That was one of the things that made his dad sort of a nerd—he liked junk food as much as kids.

"I'm fine," his dad said. "Let's stop and have a drink. What would you like?"

"A Coke," Adam replied, following him down the ramp.

"I don't think we have any Cokes in the refrigerator."

"I don't think we have a refrigerator," Adam said. He pointed to the large white container at the rear of the truck. "We haven't unloaded it yet."

"Good point," his father said, sitting down on the lawn.

"Should I tell Mom you're hurt?"

"Leave her, she's busy." He pulled a twenty from his back pocket and handed it to Adam. "Why don't you run down to the 7-Eleven on the corner and get us a cold six-pack."

Adam pocketed the bill. "Yeah, I'll just tell them I forgot my ID, but I really am over twenty-one."

"I meant a six-pack of Coke."

"I know." Adam turned away. "I'll be back in a few minutes."

His dad groaned as he leaned back on his elbows and stared up at the sky. "Take your time. I don't think I'll be going anywhere anytime soon."

2

IT WAS WHILE ADAM WAS RETURNING FROM the store with the sodas that he met Sally Wilcox. She sneaked up on him from behind. A pretty girl about his age, she had long brown hair and a sticklike figure that somehow made her look like a doll that a fairy queen had brought to life with a wave of a magic wand. It was a hot day, and her long legs poking out of her white shorts were tan and bony. She had the widest brown eyes Adam had ever seen, and she didn't look a thing like Denise back in Missouri.

"Hello," she said. "Are you the new kid in town?"

"I suppose so. I just got here."

She stuck out her hand. "My name's Sara Wilcox,

but you can call me Sally. It's easier to remember."

Adam took her hand. "I'm Adam Freeman."

Sally practically shook his fingers off. "What should I call you?"

"Adam."

She nodded to his Coke cans. "Are those cold?"

"Yes."

"May I have one, please?"

It wasn't as if he could say no, being the new kid and all. He gave her a Coke, which she promptly opened and drank. She didn't even let out a loud burp afterward. Adam was impressed.

"You must have been thirsty," he remarked.

"I was." She studied him for a moment. "You look depressed, Adam."

"Huh?"

"You look sad. Are you sad?"

He shrugged. "No."

Sally nodded to herself. "You left someone special behind. I understand."

Adam blinked. "What are you talking about?" This girl was weird.

Sally waved her hand as if what she was saying was obvious. "You don't have to be embarrassed. You're a good-looking guy. You must have had a good-looking girlfriend wherever you came from." She paused. "Where was that anyway?"

"Kansas City."

Sally nodded sympathetically. "She's a long way away now."

"Who?"

"I just met you, Adam. How would I know her name?"

Adam frowned. "My best friends in Kansas City were named Sammy and Mike."

Sally tossed her long hair impatiently. "If you don't want to talk about her, that's OK. I'm going through an identity crisis myself." She paused. "But you couldn't tell that just by looking at me, could you?"

"No."

"I hide it. I suffer in silence. It's better that way. It builds character. My aunt says I have a face full of character. Do you think that's true?"

Adam resumed walking toward his house. The Cokes were getting warm and Sally was making him dizzy. But it had been nice of her to say he was good-looking. Adam was a little insecure about his looks. His brown hair, similar in color to Sally's, was not nearly so long. His father cut his hair, and the man believed in closely trimmed lawns as well as heads. Nor was Adam as tall as Sally, who seemed to him to have stilts sewn on to her legs. But people told him he had a handsome face. At least his mother did when she was in a good mood.

"I guess," he replied to her last question about the character in her face.

She followed him. "Are you going to introduce me to your family? I always like to meet parents. You can get a good idea of what a guy is going to become by looking at his dad."

"I hope not," Adam muttered.

"What did you say?"

"Nothing. How long have you been living here?"

"Twelve years. All my life. I'm one of the lucky ones."

"You mean, it's really neat living in Springville?"

"No. I mean I'm lucky to be alive still. Not all kids last twelve years in Spooksville."

"What's Spooksville?"

Sally spoke in a serious tone. "It's where you're living now, Adam. Only adults call it Springville. Kids know the real story of this place. And let me tell you it deserves to be called Spooksville."

Adam was bewildered. "But why?"

She leaned close, telling him a great secret. "Because people here disappear. Usually kids like us. No one knows where they go, and no one talks about the fact that they're gone. Because they're all too afraid."

Adam smiled uneasily. "Are you pulling my leg?"

Sally stood back. "If I was pulling your leg, you wouldn't be standing. I'm telling you the straight truth. This town is dangerous. My advice to you is to drive out of here before the sun goes down." Sally paused and put a hand on his shoulder. "Not that I want to see you leave."

Adam shook his head. "I'm not leaving. I don't believe a whole town can be spooked. I don't believe in vampires and werewolves and junk like that. I'm surprised you do." He added quietly, "I think you *are* going through an identity crisis."

Sally pulled back her hand and regarded him gravely as she spoke. "Let me tell you the story of Leslie Lotte before you decide I'm crazy. Until a month ago she lived down the block from me. She was cute. You might have been interested in her if you met her before me. Anyway, she was great at making stuff: jewelry, clothes, kites. She was really into kites. Don't ask me why. Maybe she wanted to be a bird when she grew up. Anyway, she used to fly her kites in the park by the cemetery. Yeah, that's right. In Spooksville the park is next to the cemetery, which is next to the witch's castle—which is a story in itself. Leslie used to go to the park by herself, even close to dark. I told her not to. Last month she was there all alone flying her kite when a huge gust of wind came along and blew her into the sky. Blew her right into a dark cloud, which swallowed her whole. Can you believe that?"

"No."

Sally was exasperated. "I'm not lying! I may be confused about my personal values at the moment, but the truth is still very important to me."

"If she was flying the kite all alone in the park, how do you know what happened to her? Who told you?"

"Watch."

"Watch what?"

"Not what. Watch is a who."

"Who's Watch?"

"You'll meet him. And before you get worried, I want you to know that our relationship is not and never has been romantic. We're just good friends."

"I'm not worried, Sally."

She hesitated. "Good. Watch saw Leslie disappear into the sky. He wasn't in the park but in the cemetery. So you see, technically, Leslie was in the park all alone."

"It sounds to me like your friend Watch has a vivid imagination."

"That's true. He can't see very well either. But he's not a liar."

"What was he doing in the cemetery?"

"Oh, he hangs out there a lot. He's one of the few kids who lives here who enjoys Spooksville. He loves mystery and adventures. If he wasn't so weird, I'd be attracted to him."

"I like mystery and adventures," Adam said proudly.

Sally wasn't impressed. "Then you can camp out in the cemetery with Watch and tell me what it's like." She stuck out her arm, pointing. "That's not your house down the street with that chubby nerd on the front lawn?"

"Yes, and that chubby nerd is my father."

Sally put her hands to her mouth. "Oh no."

"He's not that bad," Adam said defensively.

"No. I'm not upset about your father's appearance, although you're going to have to watch your diet and the amount of TV you watch as you get older. It's your house that's no good."

"What's wrong with it? Don't tell me someone was murdered there?"

Sally shook her head. "They weren't murdered."

"Well, that's a relief."

"They killed themselves." Sally nodded seriously. "It was an old couple. No one knows why they did it. They must have been going through an identity crisis. They just hung themselves from the chandelier."

"We don't have a chandelier."

"They were fat old people. The chandelier broke when they strung themselves up with the ropes. Someone told me they didn't leave any money for a proper funeral. Their bodies are supposed to be buried in your basement."

"We don't have a basement."

Sally nodded. "The police had to fill it in, in case you found the bodies."

Adam sighed. "Oh brother. Do you want to meet my father?"

"Yes. Just don't ask me to stay for lunch. I'm a picky eater."

"Somehow I'm not surprised," Adam said.

3

HIS MOM AND DAD WERE VERY IMPRESSED with Sally, Adam was surprised to see. Of course, Sally kept her remarks to a minimum and her identity crisis private while she spoke to them. Sally did not have an opportunity to meet Claire, Adam's seven-year-old sister, because she was asleep on the floor in one of the back bedrooms. His father hadn't set up the beds yet. From the way he was hobbling around holding his lower spine as if he were a monkey with a sore tail, he looked like he needed one. His father winked at Adam and told him to go out and play with Sally. He said that neither of them would be doing any more heavy lifting that day.

Adam didn't know what the wink was supposed to mean.

He wasn't interested in Sally. Not as a girlfriend.

He had no desire to have a girlfriend before seventh grade.

But school didn't start for another three months, so he had a whole summer full of monsters to look forward to.

Not that he believed a word Sally had told him.

"Let me show you the town," Sally said as they stepped out of his front door. "But don't be deceived by what you see. This place looks perfectly normal, but it's not. For example, you might see a young mother walk by wheeling her newborn infant. She might smile at you and say hello. She might look real, and her baby might look cute. But there's always the possibility that that young mother is responsible for the disappearance of Leslie Lotte, and that her baby is a robot."

"I thought you said a cloud swallowed Leslie."

"Yeah, but *who* was in the cloud? These are the kind of questions you have to ask yourself this afternoon as you check out the scene."

Adam was getting weary of Sally's warnings. "I don't believe in robots. There are no robots. That's a simple fact."

Sally raised a know-it-all eyebrow. "Nothing is simple in Spooksville."

Springville—Adam refused to think of it by any other name—was tiny. Nestled between two gentle sets of hills on the north and south, it had the ocean to the west. To the east a range of rough hills rose sharply. Adam was inclined to call them mountains. Naturally, Sally said there were many bodies buried in those hills. Most of the town was set on a slope that only leveled out as it neared the water. Close to the shore, at the end of a rocky point, stood a tall lighthouse that looked out over the hard blue water as if in search of adventures. Sally explained that the water in and around Springville wasn't safe either.

"Lots of riptides and undertows," she said. "Sharks, too—great whites. I knew a guy—he was out on his boogie board only a hundred feet from the shore, and a shark swam by and bit his right leg off. Just like that. If you don't believe me, you can meet him. His name's David Green, but we call him Jaws."

This story had a ring of truth to it, at least.

"I don't like to swim all that much," Adam muttered.

Sally shook her head. "You don't even have to go in the water to have problems. The crabs come right up on the sand to nibble on you." She added, "We don't have to go to the beach right now if you don't want to."

"Another time might be better," Adam agreed.

They did head in the direction of the water, though. Sally wanted to show him the arcade next to the movie theater, which, she said, was owned by the local undertaker. Apparently it showed only horror movies. The theater and the arcade were located next to the pier, which, Sally said, was about as safe as a single plank set above boiling lava. Along the way they passed a supermarket.

Parked out front was a black Corvette convertible, with the top down. Adam wasn't into cars, but he thought Corvettes were cool. They looked like rockets. He stared at the car as they strode by, for a moment blocking out Sally's rambling. Like so much of Springville, the market parking lot was built on a hill. Adam was shocked to see that a shopping cart had slipped loose from its place near the front doors and was heading for the car. He hated to think of such a beautiful car getting a dent in it, and jumped forward to stop the cart. Sally screamed behind him.

"Adam!" she cried. "Don't go near that car!"

But she was too late with her warning. He stopped the shopping cart only inches from the car door, feeling as if he had done his good deed for the day. He noticed that Sally was still standing where he'd left her. She seemed afraid to approach the vehicle. As he started to move the cart to a safe place, a soft yet mysterious voice spoke at his back.

"Thank you, Adam. You have done your good deed for the day."

He turned toward the most beautiful woman he'd ever seen. She was tall—most adults were. Her black hair was long and curly, her eyes so dark and big, they were like mirrors that opened only at night. Her face was very pale, white as a statue's, her lips as red as fresh blood. She wore a white dress that swept past her knees. In her hands she carried a small white purse. She must have been in her late twenties, but seemed ageless. It was a warm day, yet she had on gloves, as red as her lips. She smiled at his shocked expression.

"You wonder how I know your name," she said. "Isn't that so, Adam?"

He nodded, dumbstruck. She took a step closer.

"There isn't much that happens in this town that I don't know about," she said. "You just arrived today. Isn't that so?"

He found his voice. "Yes, ma'am."

She chuckled softly. "How do you like Spooksville so far?"

He stuttered. "I thought only kids called it Spooks-ville."

She took another step forward. "There are a few grown-ups who know its real name. You'll meet another one today. He'll tell you things you might not want to listen to, but that will be up to you." She glanced at her car, then at the shopping cart still in his hand, and her smile broadened. "I give you this warning because you have done me a favor this day, protecting my car. That was valiant of you, Adam."

"Thank you, ma'am."

She chuckled again, removing her gloves. "You have manners. That is rare among the young in this town." She paused. "Do you think that is one of the reasons they have so many—problems?"

Adam gulped. "What kind of problems?"

The woman looked in the direction of Sally. "I'm sure your friend has already told you many frightening things about this town. Don't believe half of them. Of course, the other half—you might want to believe." She paused as if sharing a private joke with herself. Then she waved at Sally. "Come here, child."

Sally approached reluctantly, and then stood close to Adam. She was so close he noticed she was shaking. The woman studied her up and down and frowned.

"You don't like me," she said finally.

Sally swallowed. "We're just out walking."

"You're just out talking." She pointed a finger at Sally. "You watch what you talk about. Every time you say my name, child, I hear it. And I remember. Do you understand?"

Sally was still shaking, but a sudden stubbornness hardened her features. "I understand very well, thank you."

"Good."

"How's your castle 'keeping' these days?" Sally asked sarcastically. "Any cold drafts?"

The woman's frown deepened, then unexpectedly she smiled. Adam would have said it was a cold smile if it hadn't been so enchanting. This woman held him spellbound.

"You're insolent, Sally," she said. "Which is good. I was insolent as a child"—she paused—"until I learned better." She glanced at Adam. "You know I have a castle?"

"No, I didn't know," Adam said. He liked castles, although he'd never seen one, much less been inside one.

"Would you like to visit me there someday?" the woman asked.

"No," Sally said suddenly.

Adam glared at Sally. "I can answer for myself," he said.

Sally shook her head. "You don't want to go there. Kids who go there, they—"

"They what?" the woman interrupted. Sally wouldn't look at her now, only at Adam. Sally seemed to back down.

"It's not a good idea to go there" was all Sally said.

The woman reached out and touched the side of Adam's face. Her fingers were warm, soft—they didn't feel dangerous. Yet Adam trembled beneath them. The woman's eyes, as she stared at him, seemed to pierce to the center of his brain.

"Nothing is the way it looks," she said gently. "Nobody is just one way. When you hear stories about me—perhaps from this skinny girl here, perhaps from others—know that they're only partially true."

Adam had trouble speaking. "I don't understand."

"You will, soon enough," the woman said. Her fingernails—they were quite long, and so red—brushed close to his eyes, almost touching his lashes. "You have such nice eyes, did you know that, Adam?" She glanced over at Sally. "And you have such a nice mouth."

Sally gave a fake smile. "I know that."

The woman chuckled softly and drew back. Reaching

25

out and opening her car door, she glanced back at them one last time. "I will see both of you later—under different circumstances," she said.

Then she got into her car, waved once, and drove away.

Sally was ready to throw a fit.

"Do you know who that was?" she exclaimed.

"No," Adam said, still recovering from the shock of meeting the woman. "She didn't tell me her name."

"That was Ms. Ann Templeton. She is the great-great-great-great-granddaughter of Mrs. Madeline Templeton."

"Who's that?"

"The woman who founded this town about two hundred years ago. A witch if ever there was one. Witchery runs in their family. The woman you just met is the most dangerous creature in all of Spooksville. Nobody knows how many kids she's killed."

"She seemed nice."

"Adam! She's a witch! There are no nice witches except in *The Wizard of Oz*. And one thing Spooksville sure doesn't have is a yellow brick road. You have to stay away from that woman or you'll end up as a frog chirping in the stagnant pond behind the cemetery."

Adam had to shake himself to clear his brain. It was

almost as if the woman had cast a spell on him. But a pleasant spell, one that made him feel warm inside.

"How did she know my name?" he muttered out loud.

Sally was exasperated. "Because she's a witch! Get a grip on reality, would ya? She probably just had to look in a big pot filled with boiling livers and kidneys to know everything about you. Why, I wouldn't be surprised if she sent that shopping cart flying toward her car just so you could run over and stop it. Just so she could stop and bewitch your tiny little mind. Are you listening to me, Mr. Kansas City?"

Adam frowned. "The shopping cart wasn't flying. It never left the ground."

Sally raised her arms toward the sky. "The kid has to see a broom fly across the sky before he'll believe in witches! Well, that's just great. Be that way. Get yourself changed into something gross and disgusting. I don't care. I have problems of my own."

"Sally. Why are you always yelling at me?"

"Because I *care*. Now let's get out of here. Let's go to the arcade. It's pretty safe there."

"None of the games are haunted?" Adam asked to tease her. Sally stopped to give him another one of her impatient looks.

"A *couple* of games are haunted," she said. "You just can't put quarters in them. Of course, knowing you, you'll head straight for them."

"I don't know," Adam said. "My dad wanted his change back from when I bought the Cokes. I don't have any money."

"Then thank your dad for a small favor," Sally said.

4

THEY NEVER GOT TO THE ARCADE. INSTEAD they ran into Sally's friend—Watch. He was an interesting-looking fellow. About Sally's height, with blond hair the color of the sun and arms that seemed to reach to the ground. His ears were big. Adam saw in an instant where he got his nickname. On each arm he wore two large watches, four that Adam could see. Maybe he had a couple in his pockets that Adam didn't know about. The lenses on his glasses were thick—they could have been swiped from the ends of telescopes. Sally seemed happy to see him. She introduced Adam.

"Adam's from Kansas City," she said to Watch. "He just got here and is finding the change of scenery painful."

Adam frowned. "It's not that bad."

"What are your favorite subjects in school?" Watch asked.

"Watch is a science nut," Sally said. "If you like science, Watch will like you. Me—I don't care if you flunked biology. My love is unconditional."

"I like science," Adam said. He gestured to Watch's arms. "Why do you wear so many watches? Isn't one enough?"

"I always like to know what time it is in each part of the country," Watch said.

"There are four time zones in America," Sally said.

"I know that," Adam said. "Kansas City is two time zones ahead of the West Coast. But why do you want to know what time it is in all these places?"

Watch lowered his head. "Because my mother lives in New York. My sister lives in Chicago, and my father lives in Denver." Watch shrugged. "I like to know what time it is for each of them."

There was sadness in Watch's voice as he spoke of his family. Adam felt he shouldn't ask why everyone was so spread out. Sally must have felt the same way. She spoke up again.

"I was just telling Adam how dangerous this town is," she said. "I don't think he believes me."

"Did you really see Leslie Lotte get swallowed by a cloud?" Adam asked Watch.

Watch looked at Sally. "What did you tell him?"

Sally was defensive. "Just what you told me."

Watch scratched his head. His blond hair was kind of thin. "I saw Leslie get lost in the fog. And then none of us could find her. But she might have run away from home."

"The fog, a cloud—what's the difference?" Sally said. "The sky ate her, it's as simple as that. Hey, Watch, what are you doing today? Do you want to go to the arcade with us?"

Watch brightened. "I'm going to see Bum. He's going to show me the Secret Path."

Sally shuddered. "You're not taking the Secret Path. You'll die."

"Really?" Watch said.

"What's the Secret Path?" Adam asked.

"Don't tell him," Sally said. "He just got here. I like him, and I don't want him to die."

"I don't think we'll die," Watch said. "But we might disappear."

Adam was interested. He'd never disappeared before. "How?" he asked.

Watch turned to Sally. "Tell him about it," he said.

Sally shook her head. "It's too dangerous, and I'm responsible for him."

"Who made you responsible?" Adam asked, getting annoyed. "I'm my own person. You can't tell me what to do." He turned to Watch. "Tell me about the path. And tell me who Bum is."

"Bum is the town bum," Sally interrupted. "He used to be the mayor until Ann Templeton, town witch, put a curse on him."

"Is that true?" Adam asked Watch.

"Bum was the mayor," Watch agreed. "But I don't know if he became a bum because he got cursed. It may have been because he got lazy. He was always a lousy mayor."

"What exactly is the Secret Path?" Adam asked again.

"We don't know," Sally said. "It's a secret."

"Tell me what you do know," Adam said, getting exasperated.

"There's supposed to be a special path that winds through town that leads into other dimensions," Watch said. "I've searched for it for years, but never found it. But Bum is supposed to know it."

"Who says?" Adam asked.

"Bum says," Watch said.

"Why is he going to tell you the secret?" Sally asked. "Why today?"

Watch was thoughtful. "I don't know. I gave him a sandwich last week. Maybe he just wants to thank me for it."

"Maybe he wants to get you killed," Sally grumbled.

"It wasn't that bad a sandwich," Watch said.

"When you say the path leads into other dimensions," Adam said, "what do you mean?"

"There is more than one Spooksville," Sally said.

"Huh?" Adam said.

"This town overlaps with other realities," Watch explained. "Sometimes those other realities blur into this one."

"That's why this is such a weird place to live," Sally added.

Adam shook his head. "Do you have any proof that this stuff exists?"

"No direct proof," Watch said. "But a man on my block was supposed to have known about the Secret Path."

"What did he say about it?" Adam asked.

"He disappeared before I could ask him." Watch paused to check one of his watches. "Bum is waiting for me. If you want to come, you have to decide now."

"Don't go, Adam," Sally pleaded. "You're young. You have your whole future in front of you."

Adam laughed at her concern. He was interested in the Secret Path, but he couldn't say he believed it really existed. "I have a long, boring day in front of me. I want to see what this is about." He nodded to Watch. "Let's go find this Bum."

5

SALLY ENDED UP GOING WITH THEM, COM-
plaining all the time about how they could get stuck in a
black hole and squashed down to the size of ants. Adam
and Watch ignored her.

They found Bum sitting by the pier on a concrete
wall, feeding the birds from a pile of nearby seed. On
the way to the water Watch had stopped and bought
a turkey sandwich at a deli as a gift. Bum accepted it
hungrily and didn't even pause to look at them until he'd
finished eating.

Bum was dirty with a long scraggly gray coat that
looked as if it had been dug out of a garbage can. His
face was unshaven, his cheeks stained with grease and

dirt. His hair was the color of used motor oil. He could have been sixty, but maybe cleaned up he would have looked closer to forty. Although he was thin, his eyes were exceptionally bright and alert. He didn't look drunk, just hungry. Finished eating, he regarded them closely, searching Adam up and down.

"You're the new kid in town," he said finally. "I heard about you."

"Really?" Adam said. "Who told you about me?"

"I don't reveal my sources," Bum replied, throwing the final crumbs from his sandwich to the birds that flocked around him as if he were Father Bird. Bum continued, "Your name's Adam and you're from Kansas City."

"That's right, sir," Adam said.

Bum grinned wolfishly. "No one calls me sir anymore, kid. And to tell you the truth, I don't care. I'm Bum—that's my new name. Call me that."

"Did you really used to be mayor?" Adam asked.

Bum stared out to sea. "Yes. But that was long ago, when I was young and cared about being a big shot." He shook his head and added, "I was a lousy mayor."

"I told him that," Watch said.

Bum chuckled. "I'm sure you did. Now, Watch, what do you want? The secret to the Secret Path? How do I know you're qualified to learn it?"

"What qualifications are necessary?" Watch asked.

Bum asked them to lean in closer. He spoke in a confidential tone. "You have to be fearless. If you walk the Secret Path and find the other towns, then fear is the one thing that can get you killed. But if you keep your head, think fast, you can survive the road. It's the only way."

Adam had to draw in a breath. "Have you taken the Secret Path?" he asked.

Bum laughed softly, mainly to himself. "Many times, kid. I've taken it left and I've taken it right. I've even taken it straight up, if you know what I mean."

"I don't," Adam said honestly.

"The Secret Path doesn't always lead to the same place," Bum said. "It all depends on you. If you're a little scared, you end up in a place that's a little scary. If you're terrified, the path is like a road to terror."

"Cool," Watch said.

"Cool?" Sally said sarcastically. "Who wants to be terrified? Come on, Adam, let's get out of here. Neither of us is qualified. We're both cowards."

"Speak for yourself," Adam said, getting more interested. Bum had a powerful way of speaking—it was hard to doubt his words. "Can the path lead to wonderful places?" Adam asked.

"Oh yes," Bum said. "But those are the hardest to reach. Only the best people get to them. Most just get stuck in twilight zone realms and are never heard from again."

"That wouldn't bother me," Watch said. "I love that old show, *The Twilight Zone*. Please tell us the way."

Bum studied each of them, and even though the smile left his mouth, it remained in his eyes. Adam liked him but wasn't sure if he was a good man. The words of Ann Templeton, the supposed witch, came back to haunt him.

There are a few grown-ups who know its real name. You'll meet another one today. He'll tell you things you might not want to listen to, but that will be up to you. I give you this warning because you have done me a favor this day.

"If I tell you the way," Bum said, "you have to promise not to tell anyone else."

"Wait a second!" Sally exclaimed. "I never said I wanted to know the secret." She put her hands over her ears. "This town is bad enough. I don't want to fall into a worse one."

Bum chuckled. "I know you, Sally. You're more curious than the other two. I've watched you this past year. You go out looking for the Secret Path all the time."

Sally pulled down her hands. "Never!"

"I've seen you searching for it," Watch said.

"Only to block it up so that no one else could find it," she said quickly.

"The Secret Path cannot be blocked up," Bum said, and now he sounded serious. "It's ancient. It existed before this town was built, and it will continue to exist after this town has turned to dust. No one walks it and remains the same. If you choose to take it, you must know there is no going back. The path is dangerous, but if your heart remains strong, the rewards can be great."

"Could we find some treasure?" Adam asked, getting more excited. Bum stared him right in the eye.

"You might find wealth beyond your imagination," Bum said.

Sally brightened. "I could use a few bucks."

Bum threw his head back and laughed. "You three are a team, I see that already. All right, I'll tell you the secret. After you promise to keep it secret."

"We promise," they said together.

"Good." Bum asked them to come close again, and he lowered his voice to a whisper. "Follow the life of the witch. Follow her all the way to her death, and remember, when they brought her to her grave, they carried her upside down. They buried her facedown, as they do all witches. All those they are afraid to burn."

Adam was confused. "What does that mean?" he asked.

Bum would tell them no more. He shook his head and returned to feeding the birds.

"It's a riddle," he said. "You figure it out."

6

WELL, THAT'S JUST GREAT," SALLY SAID A few minutes later as they walked back up the hill in the direction of Adam's house. "He gets us all excited about hearing the big secret, and then he just tells us a stupid riddle."

"You were excited?" Adam asked. "I thought you didn't want to find the Secret Path."

"I'm human," Sally said. "I can change my mind." She glanced over at Watch, who had been silent since Bum sent them on their way. "Aren't you disappointed?"

"Not yet," Watch said.

Sally stopped him. "You're not trying to figure out the riddle, are you?"

Watch shrugged. "Of course."

"But it's meaningless," Sally said. "How can we follow the life of the witch who founded this town? She's been dead almost two hundred years. And what does it mean anyway? A life isn't a line on the ground. You can't follow it as you would a path."

"That part of the riddle is easy," Watch said. He glanced at Adam. "Have you figured it out?"

Adam had been struggling with the riddle since Bum had told them. But he had been hesitant to say anything because he feared he might make a fool of himself. Watch was obviously the most intelligent one in the group. He spoke quietly as he answered Watch's question.

"I was thinking to follow her life meant to follow where she went during her life," Adam said.

"That's ridiculous," Sally said.

"It's probably true," Watch said. "It's the only explanation. What puzzles me is what's so special about each place she went."

"Maybe the places aren't so important as the order they're in," Adam said. "Maybe the Secret Path is right in front of us, like the numbers on a combination lock. But you have to turn the numbers in the exact right way. And only then will the lock open."

Sally stared at them, dumbfounded. "I can't believe

you guys. You both think you're Sherlock Holmes. Bum's just taking you for a ride. He only wants you to bring him another sandwich, and then he'll tell you another stupid riddle. He'll keep going until you've fed him the entire summer."

Watch ignored her. "I think you're right, Adam," he said, impressed. "The path must be right in front of us. It's the sequence that's important—where you go first, second, third. Let's try to figure out the first place. Where was Madeline Templeton born?"

"I don't know," Adam said. "I never heard of the woman until this morning."

Watch turned to Sally. "Do you know where she was born?"

Sally continued to pout. "I think this is stupid." She paused. "At the beach."

"How do you know?" Watch asked, surprised.

"There's the old story about how Madeline Templeton was brought to earth by a flock of seagulls on a dark and stormy night," Sally explained. "In fact, she was supposed to have come out of the sky exactly where we just were with Bum." Sally made a face. "If you can believe that."

"You believe everything else," Adam said.

"I draw the line at supernatural births," Sally replied.

"The story may have a germ of truth in it," Watch

43

said. "As long as the location of her birth is correct, it doesn't matter if birds, or her mother, brought her into the world. And if the location is accurate, we don't have to search for the first place on the Secret Path—we've already been there." He thought for a moment. "It makes sense to me. Bum insisted on telling me the riddle at that exact spot. Maybe he knew we would have trouble finding the first location."

"Where did she go next?" Adam asked. "How can we know?"

"We may not have to know every detail of what she did," Watch said. "We can follow the general direction of her life. There are so many stories about Madeline Templeton that this won't be as hard as it sounds. For example, I know that when she was five she was supposed to have wandered into the Derby Tree and made all the leaves turn red."

"How could a kid get inside a tree?" Adam asked.

"She was no ordinary kid," Sally explained. "And it's no ordinary tree. It's still alive, up on Derby Street, an old oak with branches hanging like clawed hands. Its leaves are always red, year-round. They look like they were dipped in blood. And there's a large hole in it. You can actually slide inside and sit down, one person at a time. But if you do, your brains get scrambled."

"I've been in it," Watch said. "My brain didn't get scrambled."

"Are you sure?" Sally asked.

"After that what did she do?" Adam asked.

Watch started walking back up the hill. "Let's talk about that on the way to the tree. I think I have an idea."

7

THE TREE WAS AS WEIRD AS SALLY HAD described. Standing alone in the center of a vacant lot, it looked as if it had witnessed many bloody battles and been splattered in the process. The branches hung low to the ground, ready to swoop up any kid who ran by. Adam spotted the large hole in the side. It looked like a hungry maw. The edges were rough—sharp teeth waiting to bite down and come together.

"I know a kid who went in there and came out speaking in tongues," Sally said. "Snake tongues."

"It's just a tree that's been cursed," Watch said. "I'll go in first to show you there's no danger."

"How can we believe you when you come out?"

Sally asked. "You might not even be human."

"Oh brother," Adam said, although he was glad Watch was going first. There was something pretty scary about a tree with bloodred leaves at the beginning of summer.

Together, Sally and Adam watched as Watch walked over to the tree and climbed inside the hole. A minute went by and Watch didn't reappear.

"What's taking him so long?" Adam wondered aloud.

"The tree is probably digesting him," Sally said.

"How did it get the name the Derby Tree?" Adam asked.

"Old man Derby tried to chop it down once," Sally explained. "I was only five years old at the time, but I remember the day. He blamed the tree for the disappearance of one of his kids. He had like ten of them, so he could stand to lose one. Anyway, he came here one morning with a huge ax and took a swing at the tree. He missed and accidentally cut off one of his legs. You'll see Derby walking around town on a wooden leg. All the kids call him Mr. Stilts. He'd be the first to tell you that tree is evil."

"I just wish Watch would get back out here," Adam said. He cupped his hands around his mouth and called out, "Watch!"

Watch didn't answer. Another five minutes went by. Adam was on the verge of running for help when their friend finally poked his head out. He squeezed through the hole with difficulty. It was as if the opening had shrunk since he'd been inside. He walked over to them like nothing had happened.

"Why were you inside so long?" Sally demanded.

"What are you talking about?" Watch asked, checking one of his many watches. "I just went inside for a second."

"You were in there at least an hour," Sally said.

"It was closer to ten minutes," Adam corrected.

Watch scratched his thinning blond hair. "That's weird—it didn't feel that long."

"Didn't you hear us calling for you?" Sally asked.

"No," Watch said. "Inside the tree you can't hear a thing." He paused. "Who wants to go next?"

"I will," Adam said, anxious to get it over.

"Wait a second," Sally said to Watch. "How do we know you haven't been altered in some way?"

"I'm fine," Watch said.

"You wouldn't know if you're fine if you've been changed," Sally said. "You'd be the last person to know. Let me ask you a couple of questions just to be sure your brain hasn't been operated on. Who's the most beautiful girl in Spooksville?"

"You are," Watch said.

"And who's the best poet in Spooksville?" Sally asked.

"You are," Watch said.

"You write poetry?" Adam asked her.

"Yes, and they're awful poems," Sally said. "I think he's been altered."

"If I have, it happened a long time ago," Watch said. "Give it a try, Adam. I want to move on to the next spot."

"All right," Adam said, feeling far from excited about the prospect. He walked slowly toward the tree. As he did a breeze stirred the red leaves, making it look as if they were excited about his coming close. Adam's heart thumped in his chest. Obviously time moved at a different pace inside the tree. Maybe when he emerged Sally and Watch would be old, like his parents. Maybe he wouldn't get out, but become a part of the tree, a sad face cut into its thick bark.

The hole definitely seemed smaller than it had ten minutes earlier, maybe half the size it had been. Adam realized he had to get in and out quickly. Still, he hesitated. A strange odor spilled out from the interior of the tree. It could have been the smell of blood. Plus, as he stood under the tree, he couldn't help noticing how far away his friends appeared to be. They were where he'd left them, but they could have been a mile away. He waved to them and it was several seconds before they waved back. Weird.

"I have to do it," Adam whispered to himself. "If I don't, Sally will know I'm a coward."

Summoning his courage, Adam ducked his head and squirmed through the hole into the tree. He was able to get his whole body inside, and turn around, although he had to keep his head down. Standing hunched over, he peered through the hole and was surprised to see that everything outside had lost its color. It was as if he were looking at a black-and-white film. Also, as Watch had said, the interior of the tree was completely silent. All Adam could hear was his panting and the pounding of his heart. It seemed to him that the tree was also listening to his heart, wondering how much blood it pumped a day. How much blood the reckless boy had to feed its hungry branches . . .

"I got to get out of here," Adam said to himself. He tried to squeeze back out. Now there was no doubt, the entrance had shrunk. Adam got halfway through and then felt his midsection catch. Sucking in a strangled breath, he tried to let out a scream, but failed. The bark had him in a viselike grip! And the way it was closing on him, he would be cut in half!

"Help!" he managed to get out. Sally and Watch

were at his side in a moment. Watch yanked at his arms. Sally pulled at his hair. But he stayed stuck. The pain in his sides was incredible—he felt like his guts were about to explode. "Oh," he moaned.

Sally was near hysterics as she pulled his hair out by the roots. "Do something, Watch!" she screamed. "It's eating his legs."

"It's not eating my legs," Adam complained. "It's breaking me in two."

"A dying man shouldn't quibble," Sally said. "Watch!"

"I know what to do," Watch said, letting go of Adam's arms. He ran over to a drooping branch and pulled out a Bic lighter. As Adam struggled to draw in a breath, Watch flicked the Bic and held the flame under a particularly big and ugly branch. The tree reacted as if it had been stung. The branch snapped back, the leaves almost slapping Watch. At that exact moment Adam felt the grip on him lessen.

"Pull me now!" he shouted to the others.

Watch returned to Adam's side and, with Sally's help, yanked Adam free. Adam landed face-first on the rough ground and scratched his cheeks. But the slight injury was overshadowed by his immense relief. He drew in a deep, shuddering breath and tried to crawl farther away from the tree. Sally and Watch helped him to his feet.

Behind them, Adam noticed that the hole had all but vanished.

"You can see why old man Derby wanted to chop it down," Sally panted.

"Yeah," Adam gasped, gently probing his sides for broken ribs. He seemed to be in one piece, although he knew he'd be sore the next day. If he lived that long. Suddenly he had lost all enthusiasm for finding the rest of the Secret Path. "There's no way you're going in there," he told Sally.

"I don't know if climbing inside the tree is a requirement," Watch said. "It's probably good enough that we came here."

"Now you tell me," Adam said.

"Let's quit while we're ahead," Sally said. "This path is too dangerous."

"Let's go a little farther," Watch said. "I know what's next. It can't be that dangerous." He paused to look back at the tree. "I hope."

8

THERE WERE OTHER INTERESTING STORIES surrounding Madeline Templeton. Watch related several of them while they hiked toward their next destination. When she was sixteen, she was supposed to have climbed up to one of the largest of the caves that overlooked Spooksville and wrestled a huge mountain lion.

"She supposedly killed the lion with her nails," Watch said. "She wore them long."

"I heard the tips of them were poisonous," Sally added.

"Are we going to this cave next?" Adam asked unenthusiastically. He was scared of entering any more places that could abruptly close him up inside.

"Yes," Watch said. "I've been there before and had no problems."

"You were inside the tree before, too, and had no problems," Sally reminded him.

"We'll go in together," Watch said. "We should be safe."

"Sounds like a plan for disaster," Sally remarked. "But assuming we survive the cave, have you figured out the rest of the path? I don't want to waste all my time and energy hiking in circles around this town I hate."

Watch nodded. "I think I've remembered the highlights of her life. We hit the cave next, then head for the chapel."

"Why the chapel?" Sally asked. "I don't think it existed when Madeline was alive."

"It didn't," Watch said. "But she got married on the spot where the chapel was later built. She was twenty-eight years old then, and that would be the next big event in her life that we know about. After the chapel, I think we have to visit the reservoir."

"What happened at the reservoir?" Adam asked.

"That's where she drowned her husband," Sally said.

"That's what the stories say," Watch added. "People say she tied his legs down with heavy stones and pushed him screaming off a boat that was floating in the center of the reservoir."

"Why?" Adam asked.

"She thought he was chasing another woman," Sally said. "Turned out she was wrong. But she didn't find out until after she buried the other woman alive."

"Wonderful," Adam said.

"After the reservoir, we go back to the beach," Watch said. "That's where the townsfolk tried to burn her alive for being a witch—the first time."

"What do you mean they *tried* to burn her?" Adam asked.

"The wood they stacked up around her refused to catch fire," Sally said. "And snakes crawled out of it and killed the judge who condemned her to death. You remember that story the next time you get the urge to visit her great-great-great-great-granddaughter, Ann Templeton."

"After the beach, we go to the cemetery," Watch said.

Sally stopped him in midstride. "There's no way we're going there. Even you know that's a stupid idea. Dead people live there. Live people die there."

"She was buried in the cemetery," Watch said. "To reach the end of the Secret Path, we must follow her life to the end, Bum made that clear."

"Bum was anything but clear," Sally said.

"Let's worry about the cemetery when we get that far," Watch said.

"Yeah," Sally said sarcastically. "We might be ready for the cemetery by then. We might be dead."

They hiked up to one of the largest caves that overlooked Spooksville. Adam was breathing hard by the
time they reached it, and was getting hungry. From the
outside the cave didn't appear threatening. The opening
was wide; none of them would have to squeeze inside. But
the moment they stepped inside, Adam felt the temperature drop at least ten degrees. He asked Watch about it.

"Underground streams flow beneath these caves,"
Watch said. "The water in them is freezing. If you listen
closely, you can hear the splashing."

Adam stopped and listened. Not only did he hear
a faint splashing sound, but an even fainter moaning
sound. "What's that?" he asked the others.

"Ghosts," Sally said.

"There are no ghosts," Adam said indignantly.

"Listen to Mr. Realist," Sally mocked. "He doesn't
believe in ghosts even though a tree almost ate him
an hour ago." She turned to Watch. "We've done our
duty—we came here. We don't have to stay. Let's go."

Watch agreed. They left the cave without being
attacked and hiked toward the chapel. Sally wanted to
visit the reservoir first, since it was along the way. But
Watch insisted they stick to the correct sequence.

The chapel turned out to be the least scary place,
although the church bell began to ring as they walked

56

up, and didn't stop until they walked away. Sally thought the bell was trying to warn them to turn back.

"Before it's too late," she said.

The reservoir was creepy, the water an odd color, sort of grayish. Adam was unhappy to learn that all the town water came from it. The area around it was similar to the space inside the tree; it was unnaturally silent. Their words, as they spoke, seemed to die in the air. Sally wondered out loud how many bodies were buried under the water's surface.

"I don't know," Watch said. "But I do know no fish can live in this reservoir."

"They die?" Adam asked.

"Yes," Watch said. "They throw themselves onto the shore and die."

"They would rather die than live here," Sally said.

"Kansas City didn't have these kind of problems," Adam said.

They returned to the beach. By this time the day was wearing on, and Adam thought his parents would be worrying about him. But Watch was against his stopping home and telling them he was okay.

"We don't want to wander off the path," Watch said. "We might have to start over at the beginning."

"You might also be about to disappear permanently,"

Sally said. "It's better you don't give your parents any false reassurances."

Bum was no longer at the beach, and Watch wasn't sure where the angry mob had tried to burn Madeline Templeton two hundred years ago. But Watch suspected they'd tried to kill her near the jetty, because that's where the wood from the ocean usually washed up on shore.

"They were lazy in those days," Watch said. "When they wanted to burn someone to death, they didn't like to search for wood."

The jetty felt sufficiently creepy, but Adam was too distracted by the thought of the cemetery to worry about it. Ordinary cemeteries were not on Adam's list of favorite places to visit, and he suspected Spooksville's cemetery would be a hundred times worse than a normal one. As they walked toward it, Sally didn't exactly try to put his mind at ease.

"A lot of people buried in Spooksville aren't completely dead," she said. "The local undertaker is always out hustling business. If you have a bad cold, he wants you to come down to his showroom to pick out a coffin, just in case the cold goes into your chest and you choke to death. I've got to admit, though, a tour of his stock can make you get better in a hurry."

"I don't believe any undertaker could be so crude and cruel," Adam said.

"I've heard scratching sounds coming from underground while walking in the cemetery," Watch said. "I think a few people got boxed up a little too soon."

"That's horrible," Adam said, appalled. "Why didn't you get a shovel and dig those people out?"

"I have a bad back," Watch said.

"And you don't want to go digging up people who've been in the ground for a few days," Sally said. "They might try to eat your brains."

Adam began to have second thoughts. "I've had kind of a long day, moving and getting attacked by the tree and all. Maybe I should catch up with you guys later."

"Are you chickening out?" Sally asked.

"No," Adam said quickly. "I'm just stating a fact." He paused. "Besides, you've been against this quest from the start."

"It's my nature to be against anything unnatural," Sally said. "And I think this Secret Path qualifies."

"If you really are scared," Watch said, "I don't want to force you into it, Adam."

"I told you guys, I'm not scared," Adam said quickly. "I'm just tired."

"No problem," Watch said.

"We won't hold your sudden and unexpected wave of tiredness against you," Sally added.

"It's not sudden and unexpected," Adam protested. "If you'd just moved here from Kansas City, you'd be tired too."

"Particularly if I was about to visit a cemetery where people are often buried alive," Sally said.

"I told you, I don't believe in ghosts," Adam said. "They don't scare me."

"Good for you," Sally said.

Adam felt cornered and humiliated. "All right, all right. I'll go to the cemetery. But that's as far as I'll go. I have to get home right after."

"If what Bum said is true," Watch warned, "you might not get home until very late."

9

THE CEMETERY WAS SURROUNDED BY A high gray brick wall. The front gate was made of wrought iron—rusted metal bars twisted upward into points. The few trees that littered the grave site were limp and colorless; they looked like the skeletons of real trees. Adam could see no way in and felt a moment of relief. They'd have to quit. Unfortunately, Watch had other ideas.

"There're some loose bricks around back," Watch said. "If you suck in your breath, you can just squeeze through the space."

"What if we get stuck?" Adam asked.

"You of all people should know the answer to that question," Sally said.

"The brick wall won't hurt you," Watch said. "It isn't alive."

"Just like the people locked inside," Sally said menacingly.

Getting through the small opening proved easy. But once they were inside and making their way around the tombstones, Adam began to get the sinking feeling that nothing else would be easy. He definitely didn't want to be fooling around the dead witch's grave. He could see her old castle peering down at them. A tall tower rose from the rear of the huge stone building. He thought he caught sight of a dull red light glowing from a window at the highest point. The light of a fire perhaps, of many candles at least. He could imagine Ann Templeton sitting in that tower in a black robe and staring into a crystal ball. Watching the three kids who dared to defy her ancestor's grave. Cursing them for even thinking about it. She was a beautiful woman, true, but striding toward her great-great-great-great-grandmother's grave, Adam began to believe Sally's warning about Ann.

He began to believe that Spooksville really did deserve its wicked name.

Madeline Templeton's tombstone was larger than any other in the cemetery. Its shape was odd. Rather than having a cross at the top, or a half dome, the top of the dark marble was cut in the shape of a raven. The bird glared down at them as if they were its prey. Adam blinked up at the deep black eyes that seemed to stare back at him. Over and around the grave, on all sides, the ground was bare. Adam realized that no grass could grow so close to the remains of a witch.

"What a nice place for a picnic," Sally said sarcastically. She turned to Watch. "What do we do now? Wish ourselves into another dimension?"

"I don't think it's that easy," Watch said. "We have to figure out the last part of the riddle." He paused and repeated Bum's words: "'Follow her all the way to her death, and remember, when they brought her to her grave, they carried her upside down. They buried her facedown, as they do all witches. All those they are afraid to burn.'" Watch paused to clean his glasses on his shirt. "I don't think any of us can walk in here upside down."

"That's a pity," Adam said.

"You look heartbroken, Adam," Sally said.

Watch began to walk around the large tombstone. He gestured in the direction of the cemetery's entrance. "That must have been the entrance even then, so they must have carried her coffin in from over there. We should probably start there and walk this way. But I don't think that's going to work. Bum was trying to tell us something more with his riddle." Watch frowned. "Do either of you have any ideas?"

"Not me," Sally said, pacing several steps away from the grave and plopping down on the ground. "I'm too tired, too hungry." She patted the spot beside her. "Why don't you rest, Adam?"

"I think we've done pretty good to figure out any of the riddle," Adam said, joining Sally on the ground. It was good to rest; he felt as if he'd just walked to the West Coast from Kansas City. He called over to Watch, who continued to stroll around the tombstone, "We can always decipher the last part later."

Sally smiled at Adam. "Do you want me to rub your feet?" she asked sweetly.

"That's all right," Adam said.

"I have a gentle touch," Sally said.

"Save your strength," Adam said.

"We could get a coffin," Watch suggested from behind the tombstone. "And I could lie inside it upside down and the two of you could carry me over here."

"The coffins they sell in town lock when you close them," Sally said, lying back and staring up at the sky. "Remember the scratching sounds."

"I don't think we have the strength to carry you in a coffin," Adam said, distracted as he watched the dull red light radiating from the top of the nearby castle tower begin to flicker. Actually, it wasn't so dull anymore. Maybe Ann Templeton had decided to light more candles or throw another log on the fire. What did she do up there? Adam wondered. Was she really a witch? Could she really turn boys into frogs and girls into lizards? Adam couldn't get her voice out of his head. While Watch continued to poke around behind him, and Sally lay snoozing, Adam thought of the strange things she had said to him.

Nothing is the way it looks. Nobody is just one way. When you hear stories about me—perhaps from this skinny girl here, perhaps from others—know that they're only partially true.

But she had seemed to like him.

You have such nice eyes, did you know that, Adam?

Adam didn't think she'd try to hurt him.

I will see both of you later—under different circumstances.

The light in the tall tower flared again.

Candles didn't usually burn so red.

Adam found himself unable to quit staring at the light.

At the tower.

He thought he saw the shadow of Ann Templeton step to the window.

Would you like to visit me there someday?

She looked down at him. Smiled down at him.

Her lips the color of fire. Her eyes glowing like a cat's.

"Oh no," Adam whispered to himself.

Sally nudged him in the side.

"Adam?" she said, sounding worried.

"Yes," he mumbled, feeling hypnotized.

Sally shook him. "Adam!"

He looked over at her. "What's the matter?" he said.

"What's the matter with you?" Sally looked up at the castle tower. "She's trying to put a spell on you."

Adam shook himself. The red light was gone, as was the image of the beautiful woman. The structure could have been deserted for two hundred years. "No. I'm fine, really." He did feel kind of cold, though. "But I think we should get out of here." He glanced around. "Where's Watch?"

Sally frowned. "I don't know." She jumped to her feet. "Watch! Watch! Adam, I don't see him! Watch!"

They called for ten minutes straight.

But their friend was gone.

10

THEY FOUND WATCH'S GLASSES IN THE DIRT
in front of the tombstone. Adam half expected to discover a bloodstain on them when he picked them up. But they were only dirty.

"Watch can't walk ten feet without his glasses," Sally whispered.

"But he must have walked out of here," Adam said.

"No," Sally replied gloomily.

"What are you saying? He's gone."

"But he didn't walk out of here. He vanished."

"I didn't see him vanish," Adam said.

"What did you see?"

Adam was confused. "I don't know. I was staring up

at that tower." He pointed through the skeleton trees toward Ann Templeton's home. "There was a red glow coming from the highest window." He shook his head and peered up at the sky. "It seems later than it should be. Did we fall asleep?"

Sally, also, appeared puzzled. "I didn't think so. I know I just lay down for a minute. But then—I think I dreamed."

"What did you dream?" Adam asked.

Fear entered Sally's eyes. "About the day they buried the witch. I saw them carry her body in here. They were all scared. They thought it might come back to life and eat them." She shook her head. "But it was just a dream."

Adam gestured with Watch's glasses in his hand. "We have to find Watch." He turned toward the back of the cemetery, where they'd entered. Sally stopped him.

"Watch didn't leave the cemetery," she said firmly.

"Then where is he?" Adam asked.

"Don't you see? He found the end of the Secret Path." She pointed at the witch's tombstone. "He went through there."

Adam shook his head. "That's impossible. Why would he be the only one to vanish? Why not us?"

"He did something—special. You're sure you didn't see him?"

"I told you, I didn't."

Sally walked around the tombstone, talking all the time. "He was trying to figure out what the end of Bum's riddle meant. He must have hit upon the solution, maybe even by accident." She paused to consider, reciting the lines once more. "'Follow her all the way to her death, and remember, when they brought her to her grave, they carried her upside down.'" Sally shook her head. "Watch couldn't have walked up to the tombstone upside down. There was no one to carry him."

Adam had an idea. "Maybe we're looking at this too literally. It is a riddle, after all. 'Upside down' is—in a way—another way of saying 'backward.'"

Sally came closer. "I don't understand."

Adam pointed toward the cemetery entrance. "Bum might have been telling us she was brought in here backward. Maybe all we have to do, here at the end of the Secret Path, is approach the tombstone walking backward."

Sally jumped. "Let's try it!"

"Wait a second. What if it works?"

"We want it to work. We have to give Watch his glasses." Sally paused. "You're not getting scared again?"

Adam spoke impatiently. "I wasn't scared to begin with. What I'm saying is even if we do go through the doorway into another dimension—how do we know we'll end up in the same dimension Watch is? Bum said there were many Spooksvilles on the other side."

"I guess there's no way to tell unless we try it. We'll just have to risk it."

Adam shook his head. "I'll risk it. Alone. You stay here and stand guard."

"What am I standing guard against? All the danger's on the other side. I'm coming with you."

"No. You said it yourself—it could be dangerous."

Sally stared at him. "You're not just trying to impress me, are you? Because if you are, it's not necessary. I like you already."

Adam sighed. "I'm not trying to impress. I'm just trying to keep you from getting killed."

Sally snorted. "Adam, you just got here. I grew up in Spooksville. Dark doorways are an everyday occurrence for me." She reached for his hand. "Come, we'll go together, holding on to each other. That way if we end up in the witch's evil realm, I'll have someone cute to keep me company for the rest of eternity."

Adam hesitated. "You really think I'm cute?"

"Yes. But don't let it go to your head." She paused. "Don't you think I'm cute?"

Adam shrugged. "Well, yes, I suppose. You look all right."

Sally socked him. "All right? I look all right? Brother, you have a thing or two to learn about insecure females." She took his hand. "Let's do this quick before I lose my nerve."

Adam could feel her trembling. "You are scared, aren't you?"

Sally nodded. "I'm terrified."

Adam nodded. "So am I." He tightened his grip on Watch's glasses. "But we've got to try. Our friend could be in danger."

"You sound like a hero on a movie of the week," Sally said.

"I've been called worse."

Together they walked to the entrance of the cemetery. Then, still holding hands, they began to walk backward toward the tombstone. It was difficult because they had to keep glancing over their shoulders to keep from stumbling. Adam found, as they neared the grave, that his heart was pounding wildly. The sky seemed to dim more. Out of the corner of his eye, he thought he saw red light flicker in the tower of Ann Templeton. He believed he saw her image beckoning him. Laughing at him.

The tombstone rose up behind them.

The wind stirred. Dust flew. Blinding them.

"Adam!" Sally cried suddenly.

Adam felt himself stumble. No, it was more as if he'd tripped and fallen off a cliff. An invisible precipice at the edge of the world. The earth disappeared beneath his feet; the sky ceased to exist. He fell without moving. He continued to grip Sally's hand, although she could have been a million light-years away for all he could see of her. In fact, he could see nothing, not even the dark storm that lifted him up as swiftly as it threw him down. Dropping him in another time, in another dimension.

11

THE TOMBSTONE STOOD BEFORE THEM. IN a dark and dreary place.

"We've been turned around," Sally whispered, standing beside Adam, still holding his hand.

"We've been more than turned around," Adam whispered back.

He was right—boy, was he right. The sky was not completely dark, but washed by a faint red glow. It was as if the haunting light of Ann Templeton's tower had spread from horizon to horizon. The trees were now totally bare, sharp sticks waiting to scratch whoever walked by. All around them the tombstones were toppled and broken, covered with spiderwebs and dust. Many had fallen, it seemed, because the bodies they marked had dug themselves out from under the ground. Adam shuddered as he saw how many broken and splintered coffins were scattered about the cemetery. In the distance, in the direction of the castle, they heard screams, the cries of the doomed.

"We have to get out of here!" Sally cried. "Let's go back through the tombstone."

"What about Watch?" Adam asked.

"If he's here, it's probably too late for him." They heard another scream and Sally jerked Adam's hand. "Quick, let's go! Before something dead eats us!"

Once more they approached the tombstone walking backward. But this time they just bumped up against the marble. It was solid, no longer a portal into another dimension. They were trapped.

"What's wrong?" Sally cried.

"It's not working," Adam said.

"I know that, but why isn't it working?"

"I don't know. I just got here from Kansas City, remember." Another cry sounded from the direction of the castle. Off to their left, in the corner of the cemetery, something stirred beneath the ground, scattering dirt and dead leaves. It could have been another corpse clawing its way to the surface. They didn't wait to find out.

"Let's get out of here!" Sally cried.

They ran for the entrance, which was now only a heap of rusted metal. Exiting the cemetery, they caught sight of the sea, far below. Only it no longer looked as if it were filled with water. The ocean glowed an eerie green, like liquid that had gushed from radioactive mines. A mysterious fog hung over it, whirling in tiny cyclones. Even from a distance Adam believed he saw shapes moving beneath the surface. Hungry aquatic creatures. He and Sally paused to catch their breaths.

"This is worse than *The Twilight Zone*," he muttered.

"I want to go to my house," Sally said.

"Do we really want to go there?" Adam wondered aloud. "What will we find?"

Sally nodded in understanding. "Maybe we'll find this creepy dimension's counterpart of ourselves."

It was a terrifying idea. "Do you think it's possible?"

"I think anything is possible here," Sally said grimly. Another scream echoed from the direction of the castle. It sounded as if some poor soul had just been dropped in a vat of boiling water. Sally squeezed Adam's hand and continued, "But I would rather be there than here."

"I agree," Adam said.

So they headed for their houses, but it was like no walk through the gentle streets of the *real* Spooksville. In fact, they didn't even use the sidewalks. Instead, they darted from bush to bush, tree to tree, in case they'd be seen. Yet they saw no one, at least not clearly. But around every corner they thought they caught a glimpse of someone fleeing, or else the shadow of some*thing* following them.

"This place looks as if it's been through a war," Sally whispered.

Adam nodded. "A war with the forces of evil."

The houses were in ruins. Many had been burned to the ground. Smoke drifted up from the ashes, mingling with the fog that was moving in from the direction of the glowing green sea. Most of the houses, like the tombstones in the cemetery, were covered with dust and spiderwebs.

What had driven the people away? Adam wondered. What had taken the place of the people? Black shapes moved against the dull red sky; bats the size of horses screeched wickedly as they wheeled in search of living food. Holding on to each other, Sally and Adam hurried home.

They went to Sally's house first, which may have been a mistake. It was scarcely there. A large tree that she said didn't even exist in the real world had fallen across the roof and crushed the house flat. Searching through the ruins, they couldn't find any sign of her parents.

"Maybe they got away," she said.

"Maybe you wouldn't have even recognized them," Adam said.

Sally shivered. "Do you still want to go to your house?"

"I don't know what else to do. We may be trapped here forever."

"Don't say that."

"It's true."

Sally was gloomy. "A lot of sad things are true."

12

ADAM'S HOUSE WAS STILL STANDING. HE knocked on the door before entering. No one answered. Fog crept around them, glowing reddish orange like the sky. In this place Halloween could be a year-round holiday. Adam put his ear to the door, listening for talking vampires, for walking zombies.

"We don't have to go inside," Sally said.

Adam frowned. "I have to see how they are."

"*They* might be more like *things*."

Adam reached for the doorknob. "You can stay here if you want."

Sally glanced around from the dusty porch. "Why

didn't you convince me to stay on the other side of the tombstone?"

"I tried."

"I remember." Sally nodded. "Let's do it."

Inside it was dark. Big surprise. The lights didn't work. They moved through the living room to the kitchen. A roast turkey was set out on the table. The only trouble was a bunch of maggots and worms had got to it. The insects were crawling in and out of the dark meat and the white meat. Adam tried the faucet—he was thirsty. Steam bubbled out into the filthy sink.

"Cheery," Sally said.

They went upstairs to the bedrooms. Adam peeked inside his first, holding his breath, waiting for a claw to reach out from the closet and rip open his face. But there was no one there. Only dusty books that he had bought years ago, in the real world. A favorite coat a friend had given him in Kansas City was held suspended midair by a gigantic spiderweb.

"It's over there," Sally whispered, pointing to the corner.

The black spider was the size of a cat and covered with hair that stood up like greasy spikes. It glanced over at them as they peered through the door and clicked its bloodstained fangs. They quickly shut the door.

"I don't suppose we could call for an exterminator in this place," Sally muttered.

Adam peered into his sister's room next. It was also empty, except for another giant spider. But in his parents' bedroom, on the bed, he saw two shapes lying under the dirty sheet. With Sally grimacing at his back, he approached the bed slowly.

"Maybe we shouldn't disturb the shapes," she whispered, tense.

"I have to see," Adam said softly.

"No," Sally implored, grabbing the back of his shirt. Adam almost jumped out of his skin.

"Don't do that!" he hissed.

"I hear something outside. Coming this way."

Adam paused. He heard nothing. "It's just your imagination."

"My *imagination*? I don't need an imagination in this place." She glanced toward the two forms beneath the sheets. "Come on, you don't want to look."

Adam shook her off. "I have to."

He stepped forward and reached over and slowly removed the sheet.

He gasped.

They'd been dead a long time. These man and woman skeletons. Ants the size of beetles crawled over their bony arms. Their hair hung over their dry skulls like dried-out straw soaked in rust. Their jawbones hung open. Adam quickly replaced the sheet as tears filled his eyes.

"That's not my mother and father," he said, sobbing.

Sally put a gentle hand on his shoulder. "Of course not. Your parents are alive in the real world. When we get back to them, you'll see that. It will be like waking from a bad dream."

Adam shook his head. "This is no dream."

Sally suddenly froze. "Something is coming this way!"

Adam heard it now. It sounded like the beating of horse hooves.

"It is coming this way," he whispered.

"We have to hide," Sally said, getting frantic. "It's coming for us." She pulled on his arm. "We have to get out of here!"

Adam grabbed her. "Wait! This is as good a hiding place as any. Let's stay here."

She pointed to the bed. "With them?"

Adam cautioned her to speak softly. "We'll just wait until the hooves pass."

But the sound did not pass. Instead it stopped directly outside the house. "Now we're in trouble," Sally moaned.

They heard footsteps, the pounding of a human in boots on the walkway. Whoever it was reached the door and, without pausing, kicked it in. The sound of the splintering wood made Adam's heart skip. Grabbing Sally, he pulled her out of the room and down the hallway. He barely knew the layout of the house, having just moved in—in that other dimension. But he did remember there was a window beside the hall closet, one that led out onto the roof. From there it was a quick hop into the backyard.

Adam got to the window just as the thundering steps reached the top of the stairs.

At the far end of the hallway he saw a tall figure clad in chain mail turn their way.

It looked like a knight. A black knight.

In his right hand he carried a long silver sword.

He didn't look friendly.

Adam yanked the window open and pushed Sally headfirst through it and onto the broken wood roof shingles. As she groped over the slippery roof, Adam tried to squirm out the window too. But the knight was coming closer. Before Adam could get all the way out the window, something hard and heavy knocked his legs out from under him. Toppling back inside the house, he caught a glimpse of the knight raising the sharp silver sword.

Adam felt sure he was about to have his head cut from his body.

There was a flash of light and everything went black.

13

WHEN ADAM AWOKE, HE FELT COLD AND sore. Opening his eyes, he found himself in a stone dungeon. He heard someone breathing beside him and rolled over on his back. He squinted in the poor light.

"Who's there?" he whispered.

"Watch. Is that you, Adam?"

Adam felt a wave of relief. Until he realized his hand was bolted to the wall with a steel wristband. As his eyes adjusted to the dark, he saw that they were ringed in by metal bars, trapped tight in a tiny prison.

"Yeah, it's me," Adam replied. "Where are we?"

"In the basement of the witch's castle," Watch said, moving closer. He, too, was bolted to the stone wall, but he had enough slack to maneuver so he could actually reach out and touch Adam. His eyes blinked as he stared at him. "You wouldn't by any chance have my glasses, would you?" Watch asked.

Adam felt in his pocket. "As a matter of fact, I do," he replied. He handed the glasses to Watch, who had to bend them to get them to fit his face. Adam figured he must have crushed them when he was knocked out. He checked his head for injuries, glad it was still attached to his neck. He had a large bump on the top of his skull but otherwise seemed okay. His back and legs, however, were cold and stiff from having lain on the hard stone floor. "How long have I been out?" he asked.

"They brought you in two hours ago," Watch said, still adjusting his glasses.

"What about Sally?" Adam asked.

"Did she come through to this dimension?"

"Yes. I tried to stop her. Have you seen her?"

"No," Watch said. "But that might be good."

"Why?"

"I think the witch has an unpleasant surprise in store for us."

"Have you seen her?" Adam asked. "What does she look like?"

With his free hand Watch scratched his head in the

dark. "She looks like Ann Templeton, but with red hair instead of black. But for all I know Ann Templeton looks just the same as Madeline Templeton did."

"You mean, the witch who died two hundred years ago might be holding us captive?"

"Yeah. Or else Ann Templeton's counterpart in this dimension is keeping us prisoner. It's hard to tell which."

Once more, Adam remembered Ann Templeton's words to him.

I will see both of you later—under different circumstances.

"I think it's probably Ann Templeton's counterpart," Adam said, thoughtful. "I hope it is. Ann didn't seem that mean."

"You haven't met her," Watch said. "I have. She sends her black knight out to collect boys and girls. I've seen some of the kids who've been here awhile. They're all missing at least one body part—either a nose, or eyes, or ears. Or even a mouth."

You have such nice eyes, did you know that, Adam?

Adam was horrified. "What does she do with these—parts?"

Watch shrugged. "Maybe she just collects them, the way I collect stamps."

"You collect stamps? I collect baseball cards." Adam shook his head. "I don't suppose she'd want to trade our collections for our freedom." He paused. "How did you get here? Did the black knight grab you?"

"Yeah. He got me as soon as I came through to this side. He was waiting for me in the cemetery."

"Then he must have known you were coming," Adam said.

Watch was thoughtful. "I was thinking that myself. That means Ann Templeton must have been watching us from her castle and realized what we were doing. She must have been able to communicate that information to the witch on this side." Watch shook his head. "But I don't see how we can use that fact to escape."

"Were you awake when they brought you in here?" Adam asked.

"Yeah. The castle is bizarre. Besides having this dungeon, it's filled with clocks."

"You must feel right at home," Adam remarked.

"There's something funny about these clocks. They all run backward."

"That's interesting. We followed you here by walking toward the tombstone backward."

Watch nodded. "That's the key. That's the answer to the riddle."

"But when we tried to go back through the tombstone the same way, nothing happened."

"You tried to go back? You were just going to leave me here?"

"We took one look around and figured you were as good as dead."

Watch was understanding. "I would probably have done the same thing." His head suddenly twisted to one side. "I think she's coming."

14

It was not one figure, but several, who appeared through a large iron door at the end of the dark corridor. The black knight led the way, the metal soles of his boots ringing on the hard floor with a sound all too familiar to Adam. Behind him stumbled three kids, girls, all chained together. The first was missing her mouth, the second her eyes, the third her ears. But where the parts had been removed was not gory and gross. Rather, each of the girls looked as if she had been sewn up like a doll. Where the parts had been removed there was just skin.

Behind them all strode the witch.

It was Ann Templeton—and it was not.

Her face was the same, but, as Watch had remarked, her hair was red instead of black. It flowed down her back, moving like liquid fire over her seamless black cape. Also, the way she held herself was different from that of the woman he had met earlier in the day. Ann Templeton had seemed easygoing, possessed of a wicked sense of humor, true, but not scary. A pale light shone from this woman's face. Her eyes, although green like her interdimensional sister's, glittered like emeralds. She certainly didn't look like the mother type.

Across from them, the three deformed girls were thrown into a cramped cell and chained to the wall, where they huddled together, broken. The witch stopped in front of Watch and Adam's cell, the black knight at her side. For a long time she stared at them both, her eyes finally coming to rest on Adam. A faint smile touched her lips, as cold as her eyes.

"Are you enjoying Spooksville?" she asked. "Seen all the sights?"

Adam had to remember to breathe. "It's very nice, ma'am."

Her smile widened. "I'm glad you approve. But tomorrow it might not look the same to you. It might look very black indeed."

Adam realized she was talking about removing his

eyes. "But, ma'am," he stuttered. "Remember how I saved your car from the shopping cart? You said to me, 'Thank you, Adam. You have done your good deed for the day.'" He added weakly, "I thought you were my friend."

She threw back her head and laughed. "You mistake me for someone else. But that mistake is understandable. All the mirrors in this castle are dusty. One reflection can look much like another." She moved closer to the bars that separated them and put a hand on the metal. Adam saw that she wore a ruby ring on her right hand. The interior of the stone burned with a wickless flame. "I am not Ann Templeton, although I know her well. The skeletons you found in that house do not belong to your parents, although they might in the future. But none of that should concern you now. You are about to enter eternal darkness. You have only one chance to escape. That is to tell me where your friend Sally is hiding."

Sally must have escaped, Adam realized. He was happy for that at least. He stood proudly as the witch waited for his response. The chain held him close to the wall.

"I don't know where she is," he said. "But even if I did, I wouldn't tell you. Not if you threatened to boil me in a pot of water."

"You don't want to emphasize the pot of boiling water," Watch muttered.

The witch smiled again, this time maybe a little sadly. "You have such beautiful eyes, Adam. They look so nice where they are." Her voice hardened. "But I suppose they will look nice on one of my dolls." She raised her hand and snapped her fingers. "Take them upstairs. We will not wait until tomorrow to operate."

The black knight drew his sword and stepped forward.

15

CHAINED TOGETHER, ADAM AND WATCH were dragged up a long stone stairway to what appeared to be the living room of the castle—if castles had living rooms. It was a place of shadows, of candles that burned with red flames, and of paintings with eyes that moved. The dark ceiling, high above their heads, was all but invisible. While the witch watched, the knight chained them to an iron post in one corner of the room.

All around them, as Watch had said, were clocks that ran backward.

And there was something else. Something that appeared to be magical.

In the center of the room, on a silver pedestal, was

an hourglass. Tall as a man, it was wrought of polished gold and burning jewels. The sand that poured through its narrow neck sparkled like diamond chips.

Not only that. The sand flowed from the bottom of the hourglass to the top.

The witch noticed his interest in the hourglass.

She smiled. "In your world there is a fable about a girl who walked through a mirror and ended up in a magical land. The same principle applies here. Only you walked into a tombstone and ended up in a place of black magic. But you might be surprised to know that there also exists an hourglass like this in your Spooksville. There the sand flows down and time moves forward. Do you understand?"

"Yes," Adam said. "And here the sand flows up and time moves backward."

She nodded her approval. "But for you now it will stop. Without eyes, without day and night, time moves very slowly." She took a step toward them. "This is your last chance, Adam. Tell me where Sally is and I will let you go."

"Don't you want to give me a last chance?" Watch asked.

"Shut your mouth," the witch said. "While you still can. In a few minutes you won't have one to shut."

"You give me your word you'll let me go?" Adam asked.

"Of course," she said.

"The promise of a witch is useless," Watch said. "They're all liars."

"Are you just saying that because she isn't giving you a last chance?" Adam asked.

"Maybe," Watch admitted.

Adam considered a moment. "You won't let me go," he finally said. "The moment you have Sally, you'll cut my eyes out. You may as well take them now and save us both a lot of trouble."

A flash of anger crossed the witch's face. But then she smiled and reached out and touched his chin with her long fingernails.

"It is no trouble for me to take my time with you," she said softly. "And since you mentioned a pot of boiling water, I think I will have you take a bath before your operation. An especially hot one, one that will melt off your skin. What do you think of that?"

Adam swallowed. "I prefer showers to baths."

The witch laughed and glanced at the knight. "Come, we must get everything ready for our brave boys." She scratched Adam's chin, drawing a drop of blood, just before she withdrew her arm and turned away. "We'll see how brave they are when they start screaming."

Watch spoke up. "I don't like baths or showers, ma'am."

"You have no choice in the matter," the witch called over her shoulder as she strode away, the black knight following her. They disappeared into another room.

Adam apologized to Watch. "Sorry about volunteering you for the boiling pot."

Watch shrugged. "There could be worse things."

"Such as?"

Watch frowned. "I can't think of anything worse at the moment." He nodded to the hourglass. "That's a fancy piece of magic there. The witch made a big deal of it. I wonder if it actually controls the movement of time in this dimension."

"I wondered the same thing," Adam said.

A minute of strained silence settled between them.

"What are we going to do now?" Watch finally asked.

"You don't have any brilliant ideas?"

"No. Do you?"

Adam yanked at the chain that bound them. "No. It looks like this is the end."

Watch pulled at his chains, getting nowhere. "It does look hopeless. Sorry I talked you into taking the Secret Path. It wasn't the best introduction to Spooksville."

"That's all right. It wasn't your fault. I wanted to go."

Adam sighed, feeling tears fill his eyes. "I would just feel a little better to know that Sally was safe."

A voice spoke from above and behind them.

"Isn't that sweet," Sally said.

16

SALLY WAS PEERING IN THROUGH A BARRED window approximately twenty feet above their heads. She was dirty and tired-looking but otherwise no worse for wear.

"Sally!" Adam cried. "What are you doing here?"

"I'm trying to rescue you guys," she explained. "But I haven't found a way inside this stone house."

"You should get out of here," Adam said. "We're doomed. Save yourself."

Watch cleared his throat. "Excuse me. I wouldn't mind getting rescued."

Adam considered. "You're right. If she can save us without getting caught, that might not be a bad idea."

He turned back to Sally. "Can't you crawl in through those bars? They look far enough apart."

"Oh, I can crawl through the bars all right," she said. "But then what am I supposed to do? Fly down to you guys?"

Watch nodded above their heads. "There's that chandelier there. You might be able to jump and catch hold of it."

"It isn't that far from the window ledge," Adam agreed.

"Who do you think I am?" Sally demanded. "Tarzan? I can't swing from a chandelier. I might get hurt."

"That's true," Watch said. "But we're about to be boiled to death. I think the time for caution has passed."

"I agree," Adam said.

"I thought you were worried about my safety," Sally said indignantly.

"I am," Adam said quickly. "I'm just—"

"More worried about my own safety," Watch interrupted.

"I didn't say that," Adam said.

"You were thinking it," Watch said. He glanced at one of his watches. "If you are going to try to rescue us, you'd better do it now. The witch and her black knight will be back any second."

Sally squirmed through the metal bars—getting stuck only once—and crouched on the stone window ledge. She eyed the chandelier—which had candles instead of electric lights—warily. It was only six feet away, but from her perspective, it was a huge six feet.

"What if I miss and go splat on the ground?" she asked.

"It won't be as painful as being boiled," Adam said.

"What am I supposed to do once I'm swinging from the chandelier?" she asked.

"We'll worry about that if you make it that far," Watch said.

"Somehow," Sally said, "you guys don't fit the hero mold." She braced herself. "I'm going to do it. One—two—three."

Sally leaped. Her outstretched fingers barely reached the rim of the chandelier. The shock of added weight immediately pulled down on the rope that suspended the chandelier from the ceiling, which wasn't such a bad thing. Like Tarzan or Jane, Sally was able to ride the sinking chandelier all the way to the floor. The candles toppled and went out, their blood-colored wax spilling everywhere. Luckily, candles in the wall sconces still burned. When Sally was safely on her feet, she casually brushed herself off and walked over to them.

"Did you know," she said, "that this castle is surrounded by a moat filled with crocodiles and alligators?"

"We'll worry about them if we get that far," Watch repeated. He gestured to their chains. "I don't suppose you have the key to these in your pocket?"

"Can't say I do," Sally said, glancing around. "Where's the witch?"

"Filling our bath," Adam said. He glanced at Watch. "We have to face the fact we aren't going to be able to break these chains. But what if we have Sally break something else?"

"What?" they both asked.

Adam nodded to the hourglass. "It's her pride and joy. Most witches have a black cat, but she's got that. Maybe it's the source of her power. Knock it over, Sally. Break the glass and spread the dust over the floor."

The idea of destruction appealed to Sally right then. Or so Adam supposed as he watched her attack the hourglass as if she were a hungry lion jumping a plump zebra. The thing was not welded down. Probably the witch had never had an unchained guest who hated hourglasses. A few stiff kicks and the thing fell over. It hit the floor with tremendous force. The glass walls ruptured. The diamond dust flew across the stone floor.

Then everything in the nightmarish realm went crazy.

The candles on the wall sconces flickered, almost going out, which would have plunged the room into total darkness. The ground shook as if gripped by an earthquake. The noise was incredible. The castle's stone walls began to crack, the dust from the splintering stones showering down on them. But best of all, the iron pole around which Adam and Watch were bound cracked in two. They were able to pull their wristbands up and over the pole. Deep in a lower room, they heard the witch howl in anger.

"We'd better get out of here quick," Adam said, grabbing hold of Sally, his hand still somewhat tied by the handcuffs. "She sounds unhappy."

"That's putting it mildly," Watch remarked, straightening his glasses. They raced toward what they hoped was the front door. Then Adam stopped them.

"Wait a second," he said. "We can't just leave the others in the dungeon."

"What others?" Sally demanded as the ground continued to rock. It was as if the castle were being ripped apart at the seams.

"There's a bunch of kids in the dungeon," Watch explained. "They seem nice." He added, "Except they're missing a few parts."

Sally made a face. "I do hope they have plastic surgeons in this dimension."

"We have to get them out before the whole castle caves in," Adam said.

Sally and Watch looked at each other. "He's really into this hero thing all of a sudden," she said.

"We should never have called him a coward," Watch agreed.

Adam was impatient. "I'm going back for them."

Sally didn't protest. "We may as well. All we have waiting for us outside this door is a bunch of hungry crocodiles and alligators."

Just before they left the living room, Adam stooped and picked up a handful of the diamond dust that had fallen from the cracked hourglass. It sparkled in his hands like a million tiny suns. Like magic, really. He stuffed it in his pockets.

Running, they found the door to the dungeon and hurried down the winding stairway. But when they reached the dungeon, they discovered that all the cells had burst open. The prisoners had already escaped.

"But where did they go?" Adam wondered aloud.

"This hallway must lead to a way out," Watch said, nodding ahead. "Or at least it must lead to one now. I feel a draft of outside air."

"I would rather go under the moat than try to swim across it," Sally said.

"How did you get across it in the first place?" Adam asked.

"I told the guard I was a personal friend of the witch and that I had an appointment." Sally shrugged. "He was a troll. He was pretty stupid. He lowered the drawbridge for me."

The ground convulsed again. All three of them were almost thrown to the floor. Behind them the stairway collapsed in a pile of rubble. Adam helped Sally regain her balance.

"That decides it," Adam said. "We have to go the way the others went. It's probably the smart thing. They know this castle better than we do."

"Yeah, but half of them are blind," Watch remarked.

Yet they had no choice and they knew it.

They raced forward, down the dark underground hallway.

Up ahead, they could feel fresh air.

Yet behind them, they could hear the witch.

Her echoing cries. Cursing them.

17

THE PASSAGEWAY EMPTIED ONTO THE SUR-
face of the cemetery. That was both good and bad.
Good because they had to get to the cemetery if they
were to escape through the interdimensional portal.
Bad because the remaining corpses under the ground
were climbing to the surface now that the world was
coming to an end. As they ran toward the tombstone,
a bony hand clawed up out of the mud and grabbed
Sally's ankle.

"Help!" she cried as the hand began to pull her under.

Adam and Watch leaped to her aid. Unfortunately,
the skeleton had lost none of its strength with the loss
of its muscle tissue. He was one strong corpse. They

couldn't pry Sally free. Her right leg vanished up to her knee and she became frantic. Adam took hold of her arms and felt himself being pulled under.

"Don't let go of me!" she pleaded.

"I won't," Adam promised. "Watch!"

"What?"

"Do something!" Adam said.

"Like what?" Watch asked.

"Get one of those sticks," Adam ordered, referring to the dead branches lying around. "Jam it between Sally's leg and the skeleton hand. It might confuse the thing."

"I'm not that skinny," Sally said, fighting hard to stay on the surface. Slowly, steadily, Adam was losing his battle with the unseen monster. A few more seconds and Sally would be in a coffin.

"Hurry!" Adam snapped at Watch.

Watch found a suitably strong stick and stuck it down into the hole that had widened as more and more of Sally's body disappeared into it. But because he was working in the dark and in the mud, Watch had trouble wedging the stick between the hand and Sally's ankle. Finally he found his mark. Sally let out a scream. Watch was, after all, using her calf bone as leverage.

"That hurts!" she complained.

"Getting chewed on hurts more," Adam said.

"Getting boiled hurts more," Sally said sarcastically. "I've heard it all before." She slapped Watch on the back as he struggled with the subterranean creature. "Just get this thing to let go of me!"

"It would help if you didn't disturb my concentration," Watch said.

Sally slipped deeper into the hole and Adam almost lost his grip. "Adam!" she cried desperately.

"Sally!" he cried back.

"If you love me," she pleaded, "stick your own leg in the hole. Maybe it will go for you instead of me."

"He doesn't love you that much," Watch muttered when Adam made no move to offer his leg. Watch continued, "Just hold on a few seconds more. I think—Yes! It's taking the bait! It's grabbed the stick. Pull your leg out, Sally!"

"Gladly!" she cried in relief. The moment the creature let go of her, Adam was able to yank Sally free. He helped brush the earth off her as she stood up. She pushed away his hands.

"The last thing I'm worried about right now is how I look," she said. She pointed to the tombstone. "How do we get through that thing?"

"We better figure that out quick," Watch said, glancing over his shoulder in the direction of the toppling castle. "We have company."

It was true. The black knight was coming.

And with him the witch.

18

THEY HURRIED TOWARD THE TOMBSTONE, backward. But all they got for their troubles were more bruises on the back of their heads. The interdimensional portal was not open.

"Why isn't it working?" Sally demanded.

"I suppose you could ask the witch," Adam muttered. "She'll be here in a minute."

"The knight will be here before her," Watch said grimly, pointing. "Look, he's coming around that tree. We need weapons. A few strong sticks."

"A few hand phasers would be better," Sally remarked.

They quickly scavenged for sturdy branches that they could use as oversize batons. In a rough semicircle they stood guard in front of the tombstone. The knight approached warily, his silver sword drawn. Behind him, maybe two hundred yards, the witch strode rapidly through the convulsing graveyard. Her hair shone like flames. The light in her green eyes was the sickly color of death. When the knight was maybe twenty feet away, Adam ordered the others to spread out around him.

"We'll come at him from every side," he said.

They fanned out. The knight, although big and strong, was somewhat clumsy. Adam smacked his steel-plated knee with his wooden stick and the knight almost lost his balance. Sally was more bold. Coming at him from behind, she whacked the knight over the top of the head. He didn't like that.

In a surprisingly swift move, the knight pivoted.

He swung at Sally with his silver sword.

Watch and Adam gasped.

Fortunately, Sally ducked.

The knight's stroke missed. For a moment he stumbled. Watch took the opportunity to drop his stick and leap onto the knight's back. His arms flew around the knight's neck and he rode the black warrior as he would a galloping horse.

"What are you doing?" Adam cried.

"I saw this in a movie!" Watch called back, barely able to hold on to the knight.

"We have to get him off there!" Sally cried, rushing to Adam's side. "The knight will kill him."

No truer words were ever spoken. Even though they could whack the knight with their poles, they couldn't rush him directly. Not unless they wanted to be cut down by his sword. Adam and Sally watched helplessly as the knight reached over his shoulder and grabbed Watch by the arm. Slowly he began to pull Watch to the front, raising his sword in the process. In a moment, Adam knew, Watch would be missing his head.

Just then a bony hand stabbed out of the ground.

Twirling dead fingers searched left and right. As if worked by invisible radar, the skeleton's palm scanned the area. Struggling with Watch, the knight stepped one step too close to it.

The hand grabbed the knight's boot.

The knight dropped Watch and stared down at the thing.

Making an angry noise, the knight raised his silver sword.

The skeleton yanked hard on the black boot.

The knight lost his balance and fell backward, dropping his sword.

Another skeleton arm wrapped around the knight's neck.

He was being pulled under.

Adam, Sally, and Watch let out a shout of victory.

For about two seconds.

"Enjoying yourselves?" the witch asked, standing dangerously tall, only thirty feet away. In the struggle with the knight, they had momentarily forgotten her. The fire in her ruby ring flared, and a cold green light shone in her eyes. She took a step forward and smiled wickedly. "You have been more trouble than I expected. But at least now I have the three of you together."

Adam reached for the knight's sword. It was incredibly heavy. Motioning the others behind him, he pointed the sharp blade at the witch.

"Take another step," he warned, "and I'll run you through."

"Ha!" the witch said, and took another step forward, moving between them and the tombstone. "You would be no match for me if you had a hundred men and a hundred swords behind you." She raised her right hand, the one that held the burning ring. "This second I could melt you as if you were made of wax."

"I think she's serious," Sally observed.

"Perhaps we could discuss terms of surrender," Watch said.

"No," Adam said. "You don't want to bargain with a witch. And maybe we don't have to. Something just occurred to me. The clocks run backward here. Time moves backward. Everything here is backward. Maybe walking forward here is the same as walking backward at home."

"Huh?" Sally said.

"We should go through the tombstone straight on!" Watch said excitedly.

"Exactly," Adam said.

"Why did you have to think of that now that the witch is blocking our way?" Sally asked.

The witch mocked them as she moved directly in front of the tombstone. "Yes, Adam, your brilliant idea came a few seconds too late," she said. "Now what are you going to do? Search for another witch's tombstone? I'm afraid the only way you can find another is if you kill me and erect a stone over my grave." Her left hand caressed the ring on her right hand. The fire within the jewel continued to grow. Her smile broadened as she added, "A blind boy might find that hard to do, don't you think?"

Adam was sick and tired of her threats.

"I'm not blind yet!" he cried, and rushed at her with the sword.

Unfortunately, he didn't get too far.

A tongue of flame leaped out from the glowing ruby. It struck the tip of the sword and licked down the shaft of the blade. Feeling his hand burning, Adam dropped the sword to the ground. At his feet the knight's weapon melted into a silver puddle. Adam stared at it for a moment, amazed. He didn't even see the witch reach over and grab him by the throat. But he saw her eyes, oh yes, as she pulled his face up to hers. Her green eyes shone like lasers, and he had to blink to see. Out the corner of his eye, he saw the sharp nail on her free hand approach.

"I think I will gouge out your eyes here and now," the witch said grimly. "In front of your friends. Let them have a good look at what becomes of those who defy me."

"Just one second!" Adam pleaded. "I have something for you. I stole it from your castle."

The witch paused, her sharp nails now only inches from his face. "What did you steal from my castle?" she demanded.

"I'll show you," Adam replied.

He reached in his pocket and pulled out a handful of the dust from the hourglass.

The diamond dust. The magic stuff.

He opened his palm and held it in front of her face. The witch stared at it, shocked.

"You will pay for what you did to my clock," she swore.

"Sure," Adam said. "But not today."

Adam took a deep breath and blew the dust in her eyes.

The witch screamed and dropped him. Staggering back, rubbing her now burning eyes, she tripped over the head of the black knight—which was all that was visible of the poor guy. Letting out another bitter cry, the witch fell to the ground. Bony hands thrust up through the soil and grabbed her by her red hair. They pulled hard, and the witch began to go under.

Adam did not wait to see if she was able to break free.

"Come on!" he shouted to the others.

Holding hands, with Sally in the middle, they leaped toward the tombstone.

The world spun, the universe turned. The earth became the sky and the sky became the ocean. They fell without moving. They flew without wings. Finally everything went black and time seemed to stop.

Then they were standing on the other side of the tombstone.

A blue sky shone overhead.

They were home. Safe in Spooksville.

Epilogue

ADAM WALKED SALLY HOME. WATCH HAD gone off to buy another turkey sandwich and talk to Bum. Watch wanted to know if there was another Secret Path. As if the first one had not been enough for one day. Adam and Sally wished him good luck.

"Take your glasses with you this time," Adam had told him. "I'm not bringing them to you again."

As they walked the peaceful streets of the *real* Spooksville, they both noticed that the sun was almost directly overhead.

"It looks like the same time of day as when we *met*," Sally said.

"It probably is," Adam said. "I think the whole time

we were on the other side, we were moving backward in time. I wouldn't be surprised if we run into ourselves leaving my house." He paused. "Maybe we should hurry and stop ourselves. Save ourselves all the trouble."

"Why? Let them enjoy the adventure."

Adam was amazed. "You enjoyed today?"

"Sure. Just another day in Spooksville. You'll get used to Sundays like this."

Adam felt exhausted. "I hope not."

They said good-bye at the end of Sally's driveway.

"I would invite you in," she said. "Except my parents are kind of weird."

"That's okay. I better get home and help my dad unpack the truck."

Sally leaned closer and stared into his eyes. "I like you, Adam."

He felt nervous. "I like you."

"Could you tell me something? Please?"

"What?"

"What was her name?" Sally asked.

"Whose name?"

"The girl you left behind."

"I didn't leave any girl behind. I told you."

"You were serious?" Sally said.

"I was and I am."

"I don't have to be jealous?"

Adam had to laugh. "You don't have to be jealous, Sally. I promise."

"That's a relief." She smiled and squeezed his shoulder. "Will I see you soon?"

Adam shrugged. "Probably tomorrow."

Adam walked home. His parents and sister were in the kitchen, still eating lunch.

"Back so soon?" his dad asked.

Adam tried not to smirk. "Yeah," he said. "How's your back?"

"Fine," his dad said.

"What's the town like?" his mother asked.

"It's interesting." Adam thought a moment. "I don't think I'm going to be bored here."

THE HOWLING GHOST

1

THE DAY THE HOWLING GHOST KIDNAPPED
Cindy Makey's kid brother, Neil, was rotten from the
start. Cindy began to expect bad times ever since her
family moved to Springville, or Spooksville, as the kids
in town called it. At first—even though she disliked the
place—Cindy didn't believe half the stories she heard
about it. But after the ghost came out of the lighthouse
and grabbed Neil, she was ready to believe anything.

"Can I walk on the jetty?" Neil asked as they reached
the end of the beach, where the rocky jetty led out to
the lighthouse.

"I don't think so," Cindy replied, stuffing her hands
in her pockets. "It's getting late and cold."

"Please?" Neil pleaded, sounding like the five-year-old he was. "I'll be careful."

Cindy smiled at her brother. "You don't know what the word means."

Neil frowned. "Which word?"

"Careful, dummy." Cindy stared at the churning ocean water. The waves weren't high, but the way they smashed against the large boulders of the jetty made her uneasy. It was as if the surf were trying to tear down the structure. And the tall lighthouse, standing dark and silent at the end of the jetty, also made her nervous. It had ever since she moved to Springville two months ago. The lighthouse just looked, well, kind of spooky.

"Pretty please?" Neil asked again.

Cindy sighed. "All right. But stay in the middle, and watch where you put your feet. I don't want you falling in."

Neil leaped in the air. "Cool! Do you want to come?"

Cindy turned away. "No. I'll sit here and watch. But if a shark comes out of the water and carries you out to sea, I'm not going in after you."

Neil stopped bouncing. "Do sharks eat boys?"

"Only when there are no girls to eat." Seeing Neil's confused expression, Cindy laughed and sat down on a large rock. "That was a joke. Go, quick, have your walk on the jetty. Then let's get home. It'll be dark in a few minutes."

"Okay," he said, dancing away, talking to himself. "Watch out for falling feet and girl sharks."

"Just be careful," Cindy said, so softly she was sure Neil didn't hear. She wondered why the dread she felt about the town hadn't touched her brother. Since their mother had moved them back to their father's old house eight weeks ago, Neil had been as happy as one of the smiling clams he occasionally found on the beach.

But Cindy knew the town wasn't safe. In Springville the nights were just a little too dark, the moon a little too big. Sometimes in the middle of the night she heard strange sounds: leathery wings beating far overhead, muted cries echoing from under the ground. Maybe she imagined these things—she wasn't sure. She just wished her father were still alive to go with them on their walks. Actually, she just wished he were alive. She missed him more than she knew how to say.

Still, she kept going for walks late in the evening.

Particularly by the ocean. It seemed to draw her.

Even the spooky lighthouse called to her.

Watching Neil scale the first of the large boulders, Cindy began to sing a song her father had taught her.

Actually, it was more of an old poem that she chanted. The words were not pleasant. But for some strange reason they came back to Cindy right then.

> The ocean is a lady,
> She is kind to all.
> But if you forget her dark moods.
> Her cold waves, those watery walls.
> Then you are bound to fall.
> Into a cold grave.
> Where the fish will have you for food.

> The ocean is a princess.
> She is always fair.
> But if you dive too deep.
> Into the abyss, the octopus's lair.
> Then you are bound to despair.
> In a cold grave.
> Where the sharks will have you for meat.

"My father never was much of a poet," Cindy muttered when she finished the piece. Of course, she knew he hadn't made it up. Someone had taught it to him. She just didn't know who. Maybe *his* mother or father, who had lived in Springville when her father was five.

Cindy wondered if he had ever walked out to the lighthouse.

Without warning, the top of the lighthouse began to glow right then.

"Oh no," Cindy muttered as she got to her feet. Everyone knew the lighthouse was deserted. A pillar of spider webs and dust. Light had not shone from its windows since she'd moved to Springville. Her mother said it hadn't been turned on in decades.

Yet as she watched, a powerful beam of white light stabbed out from the top of the lighthouse. It was turned toward the sea. It raked over the water like an energy beam fired from an alien ship. The surface of the water churned harder beneath its glare, as if it were boiling. Steam appeared to rise up from the cold water. For a moment she thought she saw something just under the surface. A ruined ship, maybe, wrecked on a sharp reef that grew over it with the passing years.

Then the light snapped toward the shore, spinning halfway around. It focused on the jetty. Still moving, still searching.

Cindy watched in horror as it crept toward her brother.

He was already partway down the jetty, his eyes focused on his feet.

"Neil!" she screamed.

He looked up just as the light fell on him. It was as if something physical had grabbed him. For a few seconds his short brown hair stood straight up. Then his feet lifted off the boulder he was standing on. The light was so bright it was blinding. But Cindy got the impression that two ugly hands had emerged from the light to take hold of him. As a second scream rose in her throat, she thought she saw the hands tighten their grip.

"Get away, Neil!" she cried.

Cindy was running toward her brother. But the light was faster than she was. Before she even reached the jetty, Neil was yanked completely into the air. For several seconds he floated above the rocks and surf, an evil wind tugging at his hair, terror in his eyes.

"Neil!" Cindy kept screaming, leaping from boulder to boulder, not caring where her feet landed. But that was her undoing. She was almost to her brother, within arm's reach, when her shoes hit a piece of wet seaweed. She slipped and went down hard. Pain flared in her right leg. She had scraped the skin off her knee.

"Cindy!" her brother finally called. But the word sounded strange, the cry of a lost soul falling into a deep well. As Cindy watched, her brother was yanked out over the water, away from the jetty. He was held suspended, as the waves crashed beneath his feet and the wind howled.

Yet this was not a natural wind. It howled as if alive. Or else it shouted as if it hungered for those still living. The sound seemed to come from the beam of light itself. There was a note of sick humor in the sound. A wicked chuckle. It had her brother. It had what it wanted.

"Neil," Cindy whispered, in despair.

He tried to speak to her, perhaps to say her name again. But no words came out.

The beam of light suddenly moved.

It jerked her brother farther out over the sea. Far out over the rough surf. For a few seconds Cindy could still see him, a struggling shadow in the glare of the cold light. But then the beam swept upward, toward the sky. And went out.

Just like that, the light vanished.

Taking her brother with it.

"Neil!" Cindy cried.

But the wind continued to howl.

And her cry was lost over the cruel sea.

No one heard her. No one came to help.

2

TWO DAYS AFTER CINDY MAKEY'S BROTHER was kidnapped by the howling ghost, Adam Freeman and Sally Wilcox were having breakfast with their friend Watch. Breakfast was doughnuts and milk at the local bakery. Of course, Sally was having coffee instead of milk because, as she said, the caffeine helped steady her nerves.

"What's wrong with your nerves?" Adam asked, munching on a jelly doughnut.

"If you had lived here as long as me, you wouldn't have to ask," Sally replied, sipping her coffee. She nodded to his doughnut. "It's better to eat ones that don't have stuff inside."

"Why?" Adam asked.

"You never know what that *stuff* might be," Sally said.

"It's just a jelly doughnut," Adam protested, although he did stop eating it.

Sally spoke gravely. "Yeah, but where did the jelly come from? Have you been in the back room? Have you studied the supplies? You can make jelly out of raspberries and strawberries, or a respectable facsimile from scrambled brains."

Adam set his doughnut down. "I really don't think so."

"It's not always wise to think too much in this town," Sally said. "Sometimes you've got to trust your gut feelings." She leaned over and sniffed the doughnut. "Or your nose. It smells all right to me, Adam. Go ahead, have another bite."

Adam sipped his milk. "I've had enough."

"Can I finish it?" Watch asked. "I'm not picky."

"Sure," Adam said, pushing the doughnut over. "What were we talking about a few seconds ago? I forgot."

"Alien abductions," Watch said, taking a bite out of the doughnut and licking the jelly as it oozed over his fingers. "They're happening all over. Ships from other planets come down and grab people and take them into orbit for physical examinations. I'm surprised one of us hasn't been abducted yet. I imagine we would make interesting specimens."

"I don't believe in flying saucers," Adam said.

Sally snorted. "Yeah. Just like you didn't believe in witches a month ago."

"Have you ever seen a flying saucer?" Adam asked even though he knew what Sally's answer would be.

"Of course," she said. "Just before you got here I saw one come down up at the reservoir. Old Man Farmer was out on his boat fishing and—"

"Wait a second," Adam interrupted. "I thought you said there were no fish in the reservoir? That they had all thrown themselves on the shore because they couldn't bear to live there."

"I said he was fishing," Sally explained. "I didn't say he was catching any fish. Anyway, this ship came down and hovered over him and emitted this high vibration. Before you knew it Farmer's face got really long and his eyes bulged out of his head. Ten seconds of this and he looked like an alien."

"Then what?" Adam asked.

Sally shrugged nonchalantly. "The ship left and he continued fishing. I think he caught something that day, too. But I don't know if it was edible."

"But did Mr. Farmer continue to look like an alien?" Adam asked, exasperated.

"It was not a lasting operation," Sally said.

"But his chin is still kind of pointed," Watch added.

Adam shook his head. "I don't believe any of this."

"Why don't you take a peek in the back," Sally said. "Old Man Farmer works here. He probably baked that doughnut you just ate."

As often was the case when Adam was with his friends, he had to struggle to keep up. If he hadn't almost been thrown in a boiling vat on the Secret Path, he would have refused to believe this new story. But nowadays he always left the door to his mind open, in case what they were talking about might be true.

"What I want to know," Adam said, "is why Spooksville is so spooky. What is it about this place that makes it different from other towns?"

Watch nodded. "That's the big question. I've been trying to figure out the answer since I moved here. But I can tell you one thing, Bum knows the truth. I think Ann Templeton does, too."

"But Bum won't tell?" Adam asked.

"Nope," Watch said. "He said I have to find the answer for myself. And that I will probably disappear from the face of the earth before I do." He paused. "You might want to talk to Ann Templeton about it sometime. I hear you guys are friends."

"Who told you that?" Adam asked.

Watch pointed at Sally. "She did."

"What I said was that he was in love with the witch," Sally explained. "I didn't say they were friends."

"I don't love her," Adam snapped.

"Well, you certainly don't love me," Sally snapped back.

Adam scratched his head. "How did we go from what makes Spooksville scary to my personal life?"

"What personal life?" Sally asked, getting annoyed. "You don't have a personal life. You don't even have a girlfriend."

"I'm twelve years old," Adam said. "I'm not required to have a girlfriend."

"That's right," Sally said. "Wait till you're eighteen. Let your whole life pass you by. Throw away your finest years. I don't care. I live in the present moment. That's the only way to live in this town. Because tomorrow you might be dead. Or worse."

Watch patted Sally on the back. "I think you need another doughnut."

Sally grumbled, still looking at Adam. "Doughnuts cannot cure all my problems." Nevertheless, she took a bite out of the chocolate one Watch set in front of her. A smile touched her lips. "Ah, sugar and chocolate. Better than love. They're always there for you."

Adam looked away and muttered, "You should carry a box of chocolates wherever you go."

"I heard that," Sally said, still munching her doughnut, which may have had a little jelly in the center of it, too. Casually, she reached behind her and lifted a newspaper off the next table. She studied the news for a few seconds. "Oh no," she moaned.

"What is it?" Adam asked.

"A five-year-old boy disappeared off the jetty, down by the lighthouse," Sally said.

"Didn't you know?" Watch asked. "It was in yesterday's paper. A wave came up and carried him off. The police say he must have drowned."

"Drowned?" Sally repeated, pointing to the article. "His sister was with him at the time, and she says a ghost came out of the lighthouse and grabbed the kid."

Watch shrugged. "Either way the kid's a goner."

"Have they found his body?" Adam asked, feeling sick. He didn't know what it would be like to drown, but imagined it would be like smothering.

"No," Sally said, reading the article. "The police say the tide must have carried the boy out. The idiots."

"But that sounds logical," Adam said, although he was sure Sally would yell at him for saying it. Sally huffed and tossed the paper aside.

"Don't you see?" she asked. "They haven't found a body because he didn't drown. The kid's sister is telling the truth. A ghost swiped the kid. Watch, why don't you explain to Adam that these things happen. This is reality."

Watch was not interested. "Like I said, it doesn't matter whether it was a ghost or a wave. The kid's dead by now."

Sally was annoyed. "He's just another Spooksville statistic to you? How can you be so cold? What if he's alive?"

Watch blinked at her. "That would be nice."

"No!" Sally yelled. "What if he's alive and needs to be rescued? We're the only ones who can do it."

"Really?" Watch asked.

"Of course," Sally said. "I believe this girl. I believe in ghosts."

"I don't," Adam said.

Sally glared. "You're just afraid of them. That's why you're willing to leave this poor young boy to a life of torment. Really, Adam, I'm disappointed in you."

Adam could feel himself getting a headache. "I have nothing against this kid. But if the police couldn't find him, I don't think we can."

Sally stood up. "Great. Give up without trying. Next time a witch or an alien kidnaps you, I'll just order a cup of coffee and a jelly doughnut and tell whoever's around that Adam was a nice guy and I really cared for him but if he's gone he's gone and there's no sense searching for him because I can't be bothered." She paused to catch her breath. "Well?"

"Well, what?" Adam asked.

Sally put her hands on her hips. "Are you going to help me or not?"

Adam glanced at Watch, who had picked up the paper and was reading the article. "Are we helping her or not?" Adam asked his friend.

Watch glanced at his watches, all four of them, two on each arm. "It's not as if we're doing anything this afternoon." He added, "I know Cindy Makey. She's cute."

Adam turned back to Sally. "We'll help you."

Sally fumed as she turned away. "You guys are so altruistic."

Adam glanced at Watch as he stood up, ready to follow Sally. "What does *altruistic* mean?" he whispered to Watch.

"Let's just say the word does not apply to us," Watch whispered back.

3

CINDY WAS SITTING OUTSIDE HER HOUSE, slowly rocking on a wooden porch swing. Adam felt a pang in his chest—her face was so sad. She didn't even hear them approach. She seemed absorbed in her own private world. A world where her little brother was no longer there. In that moment Adam would have given anything to get the missing kid back.

But then Adam remembered what Watch had said. Either way it was probably hopeless.

"Hello," Sally said as they stepped onto the girl's porch. "Are you Cindy Makey?"

Watch was right, she was pretty. Her hair was long and blond; it reached almost to her waist. Her eyes are wide and deep blue. They reminded Adam of the sky just before the sun came up. Yet her eyes were also red. She had been crying just before they arrived.

"Yes," Cindy said softly.

Sally stepped forward and offered her hand. "Hi, I'm Sally Wilcox and this is Adam Freeman and Watch. We may not look like much, but we're intelligent and resourceful individuals. Best of all, we've been through pretty weird stuff. We believe in almost everything, including your ghost." Sally paused to catch her breath. "We're here to help you get your brother back."

Cindy took a moment to absorb everything Sally had just said. She gestured to another two-person swing.

"Do you want to sit down?" she said quietly. "Are you thirsty? Would you like some lemonade?"

"We never take refreshment until the job is done," Sally said, sitting down.

"I'd like some lemonade," Adam said, sitting beside Sally.

"Adam," Sally scolded. "We're here to help Cindy, not take from her."

Adam shrugged. "But I'm thirsty."

"So am I," Watch added. "Do you have any Coke?"

Cindy stood. "We have Coke and lemonade. I'll be

back in a second. Are you sure you don't want anything, Sally?"

Sally considered. "Well, now that you mention it. Do you have any ginger ale? I like Canada Dry best, in the green cans. Chilled but not too cold."

Cindy nodded. "I'll see what we have."

Cindy disappeared inside the house. Adam spoke to Watch, who continued to stand. He was staring in the direction of the ocean.

"What are you looking at?" Adam asked.

Watch pointed. "The lighthouse. You can see it from here."

Watch was right. Around the corner of the house, the lighthouse was just visible, a tall pillar of white plaster. At this first sight of the structure, Adam shuddered, although he wasn't sure why. He had never seen a lighthouse before he saw this one. It was hard for him to tell a normal one from a haunted one. It was only a quarter of a mile away.

"It's tall," was all Adam could think of to say.

"It's old," Watch said, finally sitting down. "It was built before there was electricity. From what I heard, they used to burn oil in lamps in the top and shine the light over the sea to warn ships away from the rocks."

"I heard they used to burn people," Sally said.

"People don't burn that well," Watch replied matter-of-factly. "Bum once told me it was the Spaniards who built the lighthouse, that it was the first one constructed in America. But it's hard to imagine it's that old."

"But later electricity was installed?" Adam asked.

"Sure," Watch said. "The waters around Spooksville are treacherous. Even modern ships have to be careful. Yet the lighthouse was closed down before I was born. I'm not sure why. Nowadays, ships don't get near this place. The last boat that did go by was a transport ship from Japan. It had hundreds of Toyotas on board. It sunk out by the jetty. For a while you could go down to the beach and pick out any color Camry or Corolla that you wanted. They washed ashore for months."

"They all smelled a little fishy," Sally said.

"But you couldn't argue with the price," Watch added.

"I'd never go out with a guy who had fish on his backseat," Sally said.

"There must've been a reason the lighthouse was closed down," Adam said.

"Probably because it was haunted," Sally said. "That's the most logical reason."

"But why did it become haunted?" Adam asked. "That's what I want to know."

A look of wonder crossed Sally's face. "Why, Adam, you're beginning to sound like you were born here. Congratulations—from now on I won't have to yell at you half as much."

"I don't know why you yell at me at all," Adam said. He glanced in the direction of where Cindy had disappeared. "She looks so sad."

Watch nodded. "Like a flower that's been stomped."

"A rose that's been crushed," Adam agreed, feeling in a poetic mood.

"Wait a second," Sally complained. "You guys aren't falling in love with her, are you?"

"Love is an emotion I only know about from textbooks," Watch said.

"I just met her," Adam said. "I don't even know her."

"But as soon as you met me you liked me, didn't you?" Sally asked.

Adam shrugged. "I suppose."

Sally suddenly looked worried, and a little annoyed. "Just don't go flirting with her while I'm around."

"We'll wait and do it behind your back," Watch said tactfully.

Cindy returned a minute later. She had two tall glasses of Coke, with ice, and one lemonade. Offering a Coke to Sally, Cindy apologized that there was no ginger ale.

"I suppose I could use the caffeine," Sally said, sniffing her drink before sipping it.

Adam gulped down his lemonade. "Ah," he said between gulps. "There's nothing like lemonade on a hot day."

"It was cold a couple days ago," Cindy remarked sadly, sitting down.

Adam set his drink down and spoke gently. "It was cold when your brother disappeared?"

Cindy nodded. "Yes. There was a strong wind—it whipped across the water, stirring up the waves." She stopped to shake her head. "We shouldn't have been walking by the jetty."

"What time of day was it?" Sally asked seriously.

"Sunset," Cindy said. "But you couldn't see the sun because of the gray clouds."

"Were both of you walking on the jetty?" Adam asked.

"No," Cindy said. "Neil was alone. I mean, I could see him and everything. I was sitting on a boulder. He had walked alone on the jetty many times before. He was always careful to watch where he stepped. He never walked out too far. It was just that this time . . ." Cindy's voice trailed off and she lowered her head. It seemed, for a moment, that she was going to cry, but she didn't. She also didn't finish her sentence.

"It was just that this time a ghost grabbed him?" Sally said.

Cindy took a breath. "I think so."

"But you're not sure?" Adam asked gently.

Cindy shook her head. "It happened so fast. Something came and took him. I don't know what it was."

"Are you sure he didn't just fall into the water?" Watch asked.

Cindy raised her head. "He didn't fall in the water. He didn't drown. I told the police that. I told my mother—but none of them believe me." She paused and stared at each of them. "Do you believe me?"

"We told you we did," Sally said, eyeing Watch to be quiet. "We just want to be sure of the facts. When you're dealing with a ghost, you have to be careful. Can you describe this ghost to us?"

"Neil was walking along the jetty when a beam of light shot out from the top of the lighthouse. It was a blinding light and seemed to be searching for Neil. When it caught up to him, old hands came out of the light and grabbed him. I know he was lifted into the air before the light went off and he vanished. I saw him floating above the water, above the rocks."

"This is what you told the police?" Adam asked.

"Yes," Cindy said. "This is exactly what happened."

"Did the police examine the lighthouse?" Watch asked.

"I don't know," Cindy said. "I told them to, but they just said the lighthouse was all boarded up, that no light could have come from it. After hearing my story, they were convinced my brother had fallen in the water and been swept out to sea. They thought I was hallucinating because I was in shock."

"A typical authoritarian response," Sally said.

"There was one other thing," Cindy said. "When the hands came out of the light and grabbed Neil, the wind howled. But it was a weird sound. It was like some evil monster laughing."

"Was it a female monster or a male monster?" Adam asked.

"That's a very weird question," Sally remarked.

"I don't know," Watch disagreed. "Personally, I'd rather deal with a male monster any day."

"My feeling exactly," Adam muttered.

Cindy was thoughtful. "I think it was a female monster."

"Let's not call it a monster," Sally interrupted. "It sounds more like a ghost." She touched Cindy on the knee. "We're going to get your brother back, no matter what."

"We're going to *try* to get him back," Adam corrected.

"As long as we don't have to risk our own lives," Watch added.

Cindy's lower lip quivered, and her eyes were wet. "Thank you—all of you. You don't know what it means to me to have someone believe me. I know he's alive, I feel it in my heart." Cindy paused. "The only thing is: what do we do now?"

Adam stood up, and with more courage than he knew he had, said, "It's obvious. We break into the lighthouse."

4

THE WAY TO THE LIGHTHOUSE WAS HARD.
Not only was the lighthouse at the end of the jetty,
but also the narrow wooden bridge that crossed from
the piled boulders to the lighthouse itself was worn
and cracked. Adam took one look at it and wished he'd
brought his bathing suit. The bridge looked as if it
would collapse the moment he stepped on it.

Fortunately, the ocean was calm. The waves brush-
ing against the jetty were only a foot high. Adam
believed if he fell in the water, he'd have no trouble
getting out. But then Sally started on her gruesome
history of Spooksville again.

"It was near here that Jaws lost his leg," Sally said as

they stared down at the water that separated them from the lighthouse.

"Who?" Adam asked, with regret.

"David Green," Sally said. "He was the guy I told you about. He was out on his boogie board when a great white shark came by and bit off his right leg. In fact, I think it was almost at this exact spot."

"I thought you said he was close to shore when he was attacked," Adam said, glancing back the way they had come. Jumping from rock to rock to reach the end of the jetty had not been difficult, but they were nevertheless pretty far from the beach. Adam wouldn't like to be out on the jetty when the surf was up. The waves would crash right over them.

"I can't remember every detail," Sally replied. "All I know is if you go in this water, you will probably come out with pieces missing."

Adam turned to Watch. "The bridge looks as if it's about to fall. I don't know if we should risk it."

"The girls weigh less," Watch said. "We should send one of them across first to see how it holds up."

"Watch!" Sally yelled. "You miserable coward!"

"I was just making a logical suggestion," Watch said.

"I'll go first," Cindy said quietly. "If my brother's in the lighthouse, I should be the one to take the biggest risks."

Sally patted her on the back. "I wish I had a sister as devoted as you."

Adam stepped between them. "Wait a second. This isn't right. One of us guys should go first."

"Are you forgetting that there are only two of us *guys* here?" Watch asked.

"Why are you being such a coward?" Adam asked. "It's not like you."

Watch shrugged. "I don't want to hurt Cindy's feelings, but I think the chances that her brother is locked in the lighthouse are lousy. For that reason I don't want to lose a leg or an arm." He paused and glanced at Cindy, who had lowered her head at his words. "But if you all want to give it a try, I'll go first."

Watch took a step toward the rickety bridge. Adam stopped him.

"I'm lighter than you," Adam said. "I'll go first."

Watch glanced down at the blue water, which had begun to churn slightly since they arrived. "All right," Watch said. "If the bridge breaks, get out of the water as quick as you can."

Adam nodded and felt his heart pound in his chest. He was about to take his first step onto the bridge when a hand touched his arm. It was Cindy. Her face was creased with worry. For the second time that day he thought how beautiful her blue eyes were, how bright the sun shone in her blond hair.

"Be careful, Adam," Cindy whispered.

Adam smiled. "I'm used to danger. It doesn't faze me."

"Yeah," Sally said sarcastically. "Mr. Kansas City grew up wrestling great white sharks in his backyard swimming pool."

Adam ignored Sally and turned back to the bridge. It had handrails that were made of rope and looked every bit as old as the wooden planks beneath them. Carefully placing his weight on the first plank, Adam took a step above the water. He had to try hard not to glance down at the water. It looked awfully cold and deep. If he stared real hard he could imagine huge shapes just below the surface.

Adam took another step forward. The bridge creaked uneasily and sagged beneath him. He now had his entire weight on it. A third step forward caused the bridge to sink even more. It was only twenty feet from the end of the jetty to the pile of stones that supported the lighthouse, but at the rate he was going, he wouldn't reach it till next month. The thought came to him that perhaps if he hurried, the bridge wouldn't feel his weight as much. It was a brave idea, but a bit foolish.

Adam took off running across the bridge.

He was inches from the other side when it broke.

The bridge didn't just break in one spot. The whole thing collapsed. One second Adam was running for his life and the next he was swimming for it. He hit the water hard and went under. His timing was bad. He was sucking in a breath when he slipped under the surface. As a result he came up choking. He could hear the others yelling, but he couldn't answer them. Saltwater stung his eyes. He coughed hard and flayed with his arms. The water was freezing!

"Swim!" Sally cried. "A shark's coming!"

Adam almost had a heart attack right then. The day he moved to Spooksville, a tree had almost swallowed him. But in his mind getting eaten by a shark would be a thousand times worse. Frantically he spun around, trying to get his bearings. He didn't know if he was closer to the lighthouse or the jetty, and at the moment he really didn't care. He just wanted to get out of the water.

"I don't see any shark!" he heard Cindy yell.

"You don't see them till it's too late!" Sally yelled back. "Adam! Save yourself!"

Adam stopped choking long enough to look back at his friends. "Is there really a shark?" he gasped, treading water.

Watch shook his head. "I don't see one."

"Yeah, but you're almost blind," Adam said.

"I don't see one either," Cindy said.

"This is a big ocean and there are sharks in it some-where," Sally said impatiently. "If you don't hurry and get out of the water, I'm sure you will see one soon enough."

"Oh brother," Adam grumbled, tired of Sally. He saw he was closer to the lighthouse than the jetty and decided to swim for it. A few seconds later he was out of the water and shivering beside the front door of the lighthouse. Now he knew why the police hadn't both-ered to check out Cindy's story. What was left of the bridge smashed back and forth against the jetty as the surf played with the wooden planks. In a sense, he was trapped, unless he wanted to get back in the water and wait for Sally's next shark attack.

"Can you feel your legs?" Sally called across the dis-tance.

"Yes," Adam called back. "They're still attached to my body, thank you."

"Try the door to the lighthouse," Watch said. "There might be a rope inside that you can throw to us."

The door—no surprise—was locked. Adam looked around for a large rock to break the handle. He doubted that the ghost inside would sue him for damaging his property.

But this was Spooksville. He probably should have thought more about what he was doing. But he was cold, his clothes were soaked. He just wanted to get inside, so he could dry off. Picking up a stone as big as his head, he brought it down hard on the doorknob. The knob broke off, and the door swung open.

It was dark inside. How clever of them to forget flashlights. Adam took several steps forward, once again feeling his heart pound. There was a musty smell; the place had been locked up a long time. His shoes left clear prints in the dust on the wooden floor. Water dripped from his clothes, smearing the dust. From the light that poured in through the door, he was able to see a spiral staircase that wound up to the top of the lighthouse. The very top was lost in shadows, and the stairway seemed to vanish into unnatural night.

"Hello," he called.

The word echoed back to him.

Hello. Hello. Hello.

Each repetition was heavier than the one before, more spooky.

Hollo. Hollo. Hollo.

Actually, it sounded as if a ghost were talking.

Ollo. Ollo. Ollo.

But not a friendly ghost. Not one welcoming him.

Ogo. Ogo. Ogo.

Adam shivered as he listened to the sound.

Go. Go. Go.

There was a small storage room off to his left. Inside was a shovel, a wheelbarrel, several metal containers that smelled of kerosene, and a rope. Surprisingly, the rope was fairly new, in better shape than the other equipment. He hurried back outside and held it up for the others to see. Watch spoke for all of them with his next questions.

"Do you want to use it to get back here?" he asked. "Or do you want us to come over there?"

Cindy stepped forward. "I want to search the lighthouse," she said. "I have to."

Sally eyed the water uneasily. "If the rope breaks, we'll all end up in a shark's belly."

"Is there a good place to tie it on your side?" Watch called to Adam.

Adam glanced back at the winding stairway. He had at least a couple hundred feet of rope in his hands. It would reach, he decided. "Yeah," he said. "Do you have anything to tie it to on the jetty?"

Watch studied the boulders. "Sure," he said. "But we'll be dangling just above the waterline."

"I wonder how high a shark can reach out of the water?" Sally muttered.

Adam threw one end of the rope over to Watch, who wrapped it around a boulder. Before Watch tied his end off, Adam reentered the lighthouse and secured his end to the stairway. He knew it was ridiculous, but he thought he heard his *hello* still echoing. It was only a faint moan though.

Oooooo.

Adam went back outside. Watch had drawn the rope tight and tied it. It stretched only three feet above the water. "Who's going first?" Adam called.

Cindy grabbed hold of the rope. "I will." Then she paused. "What do I do?"

"Start with your back to the lighthouse," Watch explained. "Grab the rope tightly with your hands and pull yourself out slowly. When you're above the water, throw your feet around the rope, too. And don't fall off."

Cindy did what Watch instructed. Soon she was inching her way toward Adam. The ends of her blond hair brushed the tips of the small waves. Adam wanted to say something to encourage her, but couldn't think of anything—especially with Sally glaring at him.

Adam just didn't understand Sally. She had been the one who wanted to help Cindy in the first place. Just because he said a few nice things about Cindy was no reason for Sally to get so jealous. Adam didn't even know what there was to be jealous about. They were kids and weren't into relationships. He wasn't even sure what the word meant.

"Just a few more feet," Adam said finally when Cindy was almost across. When her feet were above the stones, he reached out and helped her off the rope. She stood beside him and caught her breath.

"That was scary," she said.

"How long have you lived in Spooksville?" he asked.

"Two months. How about you?"

"Two weeks. We moved because of my dad's job."

Cindy's face fell. "We moved because my dad died."

"Oh. I'm sorry."

"His family had a house here that we stay in for free." Cindy shrugged weakly. "We had nowhere else to go."

"You don't have any other brothers or sisters? Besides Neil?"

"No."

"Hey!" Sally called from across the water, her hand on the rope. "Stop talking and get ready to rescue me if I fall in."

"I can't wait to rescue you again," Adam called back.

Sally took longer to cross than Cindy. Actually, she complained so much the whole way it was amazing she had enough strength left to hold on to the rope. But finally she was standing beside them.

"I hope we're not in a hurry on the way back," Sally said.

Watch was over in a few moments. The rope was strong; it hardly even sagged under Watch's weight. As long as there were no great whites in the area, they decided, they should have a safe return trip.

As a group, they entered the lighthouse. The ground floor was basically empty. Except for the storage area, and a bunch of spider webs, there was only dust. The spiral stairway seemed to wait for them, daring them, if they had the nerve, to climb its many steps into darkness. Adam gestured above.

"I wish we had at least one flashlight," he said.

"When we left home we were just going for doughnuts," Watch said. He tested the metal steps with both his hands. "The stairway appears strong enough. I bet it leads up to a door of some kind."

"Why do you say that?" Sally asked.

"It's dark in here," Watch explained. "But the lighthouse windows are not boarded up. You can see that from the outside. There must be a floor of some kind above us that blocks us from the windows." He stepped onto the stairway. "I guess we'll see in a few minutes."

"Should we go up together?" Sally asked, glancing around nervously.

"You can stay here all by yourself," Adam said, following Watch onto the steps. "But you've seen enough horror films to know what happens when you're all alone in a dark place."

"I grew up in this town," Sally snapped. "I watch horror films to relax before I go to sleep." She put a foot onto the stairway. "I just hope these steps don't suddenly end."

"It would be a long fall," Watch agreed, taking the lead.

"I just hope my brother's up there," Cindy said quietly, walking a step behind Adam.

The hike up the stairs was very hard. They were panting within a few minutes. And the floor looked so far away so quickly; it made Adam dizzy to look down. Also, it was unnerving to climb into blackness. Occasionally a spider web would settle over their faces and make them jump. Adam wished he had a Bic lighter or something to see with. The higher they climbed, the darker it got, and the warmer. Adam was about to call for Watch to stop and rest when Watch shouted, "Ouch!" He was practically invisible in the dark.

"We've reached the top," Watch said, rubbing the top of his head.

"Is there a door?" Sally asked, crowding up between Adam and Cindy.

"I smashed my head against something—I hope it's a door," Watch said. "Stay cool, I'm about to pound it with my fist to try to open it."

Watch pounded on what sounded like a wooden door several times without success.

"You might want to use your head," Sally suggested. "You had better luck with it."

"Maybe there's a lock," Cindy said, slipping past Adam, who could hardly see her. Adam listened for a moment while Watch and Cindy ran their fingers over the wooden door above them. Then suddenly there was a click and a ray of light struck Adam's face. It was coming from outside, through the windows at the top of the lighthouse. Cindy and Watch had pushed open the trapdoor.

As a group, they climbed into the top of the lighthouse.

It was dusty as well, and there were cobwebs everywhere. The dust lay particularly thick on the huge metal mirror that curved behind the giant searchlight that stood in the center of the room. Watch drew his finger over the mirror, and Adam was surprised to see how shiny the metal was beneath the dust. The twin bulbs that formed the heart of the searchlight were not covered by glass; they bulged near the center of the mirror like two watchful eyes. Watch studied the searchlight for a moment, checking on the wires that led to it.

"This thing hasn't been turned on in years," he said finally.

Cindy was disturbed. "It came on two days ago."

"Are you sure the light came from here?" Adam asked.

"Positive," Cindy said.

Watch was doubtful. "These wires are worn. I don't think they're capable of carrying an electrical current."

"I know what I saw," Cindy insisted. She scanned the rest of the room. "He must be here somewhere," she said softly, desperately.

Adam tried to make her feel better. "If a ghost did take your brother, it might have taken him somewhere else."

Cindy sighed. "So, you're saying he could be anywhere, which is the same as saying we're never going to find him."

"No," Adam said quickly. "I meant we've only begun to search. Let's look around some more."

There wasn't much to the room. Besides the search-light, there was a plain wooden desk and chair, a simple cot, and a bathroom that looked as if it hadn't been used in years. The faucet in the sink didn't even work. When they tried it, a faint smell of gas came out instead of water.

But Sally did find something unusual on one side of the desk. Carved in the old wood, on opposite sides of a roughly shaped heart, were two words: *Mommy* and *Rick.* The words were probably carved by a child. Adam looked to Sally and Watch.

"Do you know who operated the lighthouse last?" Adam asked.

"I heard it was a bloodsucking sailor," Sally said.

Watch shook his head. "No. The bloodsucker was the guy who used to run the bait shop on the pier. Bum said the lighthouse was last run by a woman—an old woman."

"Is she dead now?" Cindy asked.

"Most old people in Spooksville are dead," Sally said.

Watch nodded. "This was at least thirty years ago. I'm sure the woman is dead."

"You have to be dead to be a ghost," Sally said, trying to encourage Cindy.

"What about this Rick?" Adam asked.

Watch shook his head. "I don't know what happened to him. Bum might, if we can find him. There might also be records in the library that we could check."

Sally made a face. "We have to go to the library? Yuck!"

"What's wrong with the library?" Adam asked reluctantly.

"The librarian's a little strange," Watch said.

"A little?" Sally said. "His name's Mr. Spiney and when he takes your picture for your library card, he actually takes an X-ray. He likes to see your bones when you check out a book, to make sure they're healthy. If you go in the reference room, he locks you inside. Just in case you're thinking of stealing one of his precious magazines or papers. The last time I went in there I was a prisoner for two nights before he let me out. I read the last ten years of *Time* magazine and *Fangoria*."

"I'm glad you put the time to good use," Watch said.

"Mr. Spiney also forces you to drink milk when you're at the library," Sally said. "'Don't want to let those bones crumble before their time,' he always says. I swear I saw that guy at the cemetery once digging up skeletons. I hear he's got a whole closet full of bones at home."

"Let's not worry about Mr. Spiney," Adam said, not wanting to listen to another weird Sally-Watch conversation. "I want to go to the library." He paused and turned to Cindy. "As long as that's all right with you?"

Cindy nodded sadly, still looking around. "I was hoping so hard I'd find Neil here, waiting for me."

Adam patted her on the back. "We're making progress. That's what's important."

They started to follow Watch down the stairs.

It was then that the searchlight came on.

By mysterious chance, the light was pointed not out to sea but toward the stairway. Watch was already several steps down the stairs when the light blazed to life, but Cindy was just stepping down into it. Like the rest of them, the sudden light blinded Cindy. Rather than stepping onto the stairway, she stumbled and slid over the side. Adam saw a falling blur off to his left and heard her scream. Not sure what he was doing, he dove to catch her.

The searchlight went off.

Adam saw stars, not much else. But after a second or two he realized he was holding on to one of Cindy's hands, and that she was struggling desperately at the end of it. If she let go, or if he let go of her, she would plunge over a hundred feet to the floor of the lighthouse. Adam screamed for Watch to help.

"Pull her over toward you on the stairway!" Adam called.

"I can't reach her!" Watch shouted back, cleaning his glasses on his shirt. He did have the worst eyes of all of them.

"I'm right here!" Cindy cried. The trapdoor that led into the upper room was fairly wide. Cindy had stumbled off the side opposite the stairway. As Adam's vision cleared, he saw her feet kicking in midair. Sally kneeled by his side and tried to grab Cindy's other hand.

"We won't let you go!" Sally cried.

"You're knocking my hand loose!" Cindy screamed.

"Oh," Sally said, and sat back on her knees. "Sorry."

"Watch," Adam said anxiously, losing his grip on Cindy, "put your glasses back on and reach out and grab her feet. I'm going to lose her."

Watch rubbed his eyes. "I really can't see yet. Cindy, keep talking or screaming or something. I'll hone in on you."

"Okay, I can talk," Cindy said breathlessly. "What should I talk about? I've always been afraid of heights. I don't like ghosts much either. But I like ice cream. I like school. I like singing. Some boys."

"Which boys?" Sally asked, climbing back up on her knees.

"Gotcha," Watch said, reaching out and grabbing Cindy's feet.

"Are you sure you've got her?" Adam asked.

"Don't let go of her yet if that's what you're asking," Watch said, pulling Cindy closer.

"That's exactly what he's asking," Cindy said frantically. But just then her feet touched something solid "Oh. Thank goodness. Is that the stairs below my feet?"

"It better be," Watch said, pulling Cindy farther over. "It's what I'm standing on. But I still can't see." Watch pulled her all the way on the stairs. "You're safe."

Adam let go of Cindy's hand. "Whew," he said. "That was close." He turned back toward the searchlight and complained to Watch. "I thought you said the light couldn't come on?"

Watch came back up the steps, Cindy by his side. Watch studied the wires that led to the searchlight, but once more shook his head.

"Did you guys touch anything?" Watch asked.

"No," Adam and Sally said.

"I don't see how it turned on," Watch said. "These wires are shot."

"Could it have another source of power?" Cindy wondered aloud.

They all looked at one another.

Then they heard a sound.

A faint howling sound.

It seemed to come from far off. From somewhere out over the ocean. But it wasn't so far away that it didn't scare them. They hurried down the stairs and out of the lighthouse. Actually, they ran out of the place and worked their way back to the jetty on the rope. They could check it out later, they decided.

5

WATCH COULDN'T FIND BUM, SO THEY ENDED up at the library. To Adam, the place looked more like a ghost house than a place for books. But he was getting used to such things since moving to Spooksville.

Mr. Spiney met them at the door. He had to be the thinnest man Adam had ever seen. Tall and bent, he looked as if his skinny bones were about to burst through his wrinkled skin. He had large hands that looked like claws. He wore an outdated black suit, with vest, and he bowed slightly as he let them inside his library. His voice, when he spoke, made him sound like an old fish.

"Hello children, and welcome," he said. "I do hope

your hands are clean and your minds are not dirty. Would you like a glass of milk?"

"No thank you," Sally said quickly. "We're just here to check a few reference materials."

"Sally Wilcox," Mr. Spiney said, peering a little closer. "How nice of you to visit me again." He reached out with one of his clawlike hands. "How are your bones feeling these days?"

Sally took a step back. "Fine, thank you. We don't want any milk and our bones are all perfectly hard and strong. Can we please look at your old newspapers? And can you promise not to lock us inside the reference room?"

Mr. Spiney took a step back and eyed them with a trace of suspicion. "What are you going to do with my newspapers?"

"Just read them," Watch said. "But I wouldn't mind a glass of milk."

Mr. Spiney smiled and nodded. "If you don't drink your milk, you're bound to get osteoporosis." He looked at Cindy and Adam. "Do you know what that is?"

"No," Cindy said.

"And we don't want to know," Adam said.

Mr. Spiney huffed. "Very well. But don't come running to me when your bones begin to crumble. It will be much too late then."

Mr. Spiney led them to a dark room located on the second floor of the library, and then he went to fetch Watch's milk. Sally, of course, believed the milk would be poisonous, but Watch said he was thirsty and didn't care.

Spooksville's official paper was called *The Daily Disaster*. Adam was amazed by how large the obituary section was for such a small town. In each issue, it took up half the paper. Sally was right about one thing: not everyone stayed for long in Spooksville. The cause of death was often listed as simply *disappeared*.

Watch believed they should start searching for information about the lighthouse from thirty years ago.

"Do you know for sure that it closed then?" Cindy asked, helping him get the papers down from the shelves.

"According to Bum it was about then," Watch said.

"What are we looking for anyway?" Sally grumbled. "They don't write about ghosts in the paper. Not even in *The Daily Disaster*."

"I assume we're looking for the person who turned into the ghost that stole Cindy's brother," Adam said. He glanced at Watch. "Is that right?"

Watch nodded. "I'd be happy to find out who Mommy and Rick were," Watch replied, spreading the papers out on a table in the center of the small dark room.

They searched the papers for more than an hour. During that time Mr. Spiney appeared three times with glasses of milk for everyone. Sally refused to drink any, but Adam and Cindy finally decided to have a little so they wouldn't be rude. Mr. Spiney stood nearby while they sipped. Adam made a face and almost spit out his milk.

"This tastes like it's got sand in it," he complained.

"It's not sand," Mr. Spiney explained. "It's calcium powder. It will make your bones so hard that even when you've been dead and buried twenty years, they'll still be nice and white." He grinned at Cindy and Adam, and for the first time they both noticed what big teeth Mr. Spiney had. "You'll both make beautiful corpses," he said with feeling.

Cindy set her glass down and coughed. "I think I'm getting a milk allergy."

Mr. Spiney finally left them alone, and not long after that Watch uncovered a paper that had an article about the lighthouse.

Double Tragedy at Sea

Last Saturday there was a power failure at the lighthouse. Not long afterward a ship, the *Halifax*, smashed into the reef off Springville and sank. Its captain was listed as Dwayne

Pillar. Captain Pillar went down with his ship; his body has yet to be found. What caused the power failure at the lighthouse has not been determined. But the absence of a light was clearly responsible for the wreck of the ship.

By unfortunate chance, the following evening the son of Mrs. Evelyn Maey, the lighthouse keeper, was playing on the jetty beside the lighthouse when a wave washed him out to sea. Five-year-old Rick has yet to be found, and the authorities fear he has drowned. Evelyn Maey was unavailable for comment.

"That's it!" Sally exclaimed.

Everyone looked at her. "What's it?" Watch finally asked.

Sally was excited. "Don't you see? The ghost of Captain Pillar stole Rick because his mother messed up the searchlight and caused the captain's ship to crash. It was his way of getting back at her."

Watch nodded. "That's logical. But what does this ghost have to do with Neil?"

"Yeah," Adam said. "He didn't do anything to the sailor."

Sally spoke with strained patience. "That doesn't

matter. Rick was five years old. Neil was five years old. The sailor ghost just likes five-year-old boys. Also, note the time of day Rick was swiped. Near sunset. It was the same time of day Neil disappeared."

"Those are a lot of coincidences," Adam admitted.

"But I thought the old woman's ghost stole Neil," Cindy said.

"What made you think that?" Sally asked.

"Because the ghost that grabbed Neil had hands like an old woman," Cindy said. "She howled like one, too."

"Since when do old women howl?" Sally asked. "Look, we have a clear case of a ghost snatching a boy just like your brother. It's got to be the same ghost. I'd bet my reputation on it."

"That doesn't exactly make you a heavy bettor," Adam muttered.

"Where do you think this sailor ghost is?" Cindy asked, ignoring him.

"He probably lives out on his ship," Sally said.

"Which just happens to be sunk underwater," Adam remarked.

Watch was thoughtful. "But that doesn't mean we can't get to the ship, and that it wouldn't have an air space in it that a person could survive in for a few days. Neil could be there, and alive. They say the *Titanic* had whole rooms that the water didn't get into. And that was underwater a whole lot longer than this ship."

"How do we get to the ship?" Adam asked. "And wouldn't we need scuba equipment?"

"I have scuba equipment," Watch said. "I've been diving since I was seven."

"But you can't dive alone in that shark-infested water," Sally said. "It's not safe."

"I have plenty of equipment," Watch said. "I'll take Adam with me."

"But I don't know how to dive," Adam protested.

"I'll teach you," Watch said. "I have a diving certificate. You'll see. It's a lot of fun."

"What if a shark does come?" Cindy asked, although she was clearly excited that they might find her brother.

"He can eat only one of us at a time," Watch said cheerfully.

6

ANOTHER HOUR OR SO PASSED BEFORE they were able to haul the scuba equipment to the end of the jetty. Adam couldn't believe how heavy the air tanks were. They ended up borrowing a shopping cart from the supermarket to push some of the stuff. But they couldn't take the cart out on the rocky jetty. Adam was exhausted before getting in the water.

"I need to rest," Adam said as he set the tank down next to the rope they had tied to the lighthouse. The equipment looked so complex, he didn't see how he was going to learn to use it in a few minutes. Plus, he couldn't stop thinking about sharks. He didn't want to go through the rest of his life with a nickname like Jaws.

"That might not be a good idea," Watch said. "It's getting late. You want to dive with as much sunlight as possible. The sooner we get in the water the better."

Adam gestured to the equipment. "Will you really be able to teach me how to use all this?"

"You're not chickening out, are you?" Sally asked sweetly.

Adam started to defend himself when Cindy stepped forward and spoke up for him. "Adam's no chicken," she said. "He was the first one to cross over to the lighthouse, in case you've forgotten."

Sally didn't like being challenged by a girl, even one she was supposedly trying to help. She shook a finger in Cindy's face.

"You just remember that it was me who started this whole rescue operation," Sally said. "Besides, Adam and I have been friends a long time. I can call him chicken whenever I want. And he accepts it."

"I wouldn't go that far," Adam said.

"And he's only lived here two weeks," Watch added.

"I just feel like you're jealous of me or something," Cindy said to Sally.

Sally snorted. "Why would I be jealous of you?"

"Cindy should be asking you that question," Adam said.

Sally exploded. "Why do you always take her side?"

"I told you, the sooner we get in the water the bet- ter," Watch said.

"I am not always taking her side," Adam said to Sally. "I just think you need to relax a little. That's all. Take things as they come."

Sally smoldered. "We'll see how relaxed you are when a great white shows up."

While getting the scuba equipment at Watch's house, Adam and Watch had picked up swimming trunks. Climb- ing into the scuba gear, Adam kept asking about each piece of equipment. Watch held up his hand to reassure him.

"I'll adjust all your equipment," Watch said. "All you have to remember is to breathe through your mouth. And don't rush to the surface."

"What happens if I choke and need to get to the surface fast?" Adam asked.

"Your lungs will explode and your face mask will fill with blood," Watch said. "If you choke, cough into your regulator."

"What's that?"

"The thing that goes in your mouth. Also, if you need to clear your mask, hold the top with one hand and blow out through your nose. The air pressure will expel the water."

Adam was getting nervous. "Does the mask usually fill with water?"

"It can," Watch said.

"Then you couldn't see around you," Sally said darkly. "What's coming for you."

Watch lifted one of the air tanks onto Adam's back. Adam felt as if he were on Jupiter, where gravity was four times greater than on Earth. He could hardly move.

"As soon as you get in the water, you won't feel the weight at all," Watch said. He pointed a hundred yards out to sea. "See where the water changes color right there?"

"Yes," Adam said, panting. Where Watch pointed, the water was a lighter blue.

"That's the beginning of the reef," Watch said. "The ship's probably wrecked somewhere near there. But the reef runs out a quarter mile. We might have to search for a while."

"How long will our air last?" Adam asked, checking the gauge. It read 3000 psi. He hadn't a clue what that meant.

"An hour, if we don't go too deep," Watch said. "When it says zero psi, you're out of air."

"What do we do if we see a shark?" Adam asked.

"Pray," Sally said.

"Go to the bottom," Watch said. "And pray."

Just before Adam climbed in the water, Cindy leaned over and kissed him on the cheek. He had never been kissed by a girl before except his mother, who didn't count. He didn't know what he was supposed to do. He was too scared to kiss her back, especially in front of Sally, who suddenly looked a lot like a shark herself. He just smiled and tried to give her hope.

"Maybe we'll find your brother," Adam said.

Cindy spoke simply, staring at him. "I know you'll find him, Adam."

"Oh brother," Sally muttered. "He'll be lucky if he comes back in one piece." But then Sally acted concerned and touched Adam's arm. "You know, I'm kidding. You be careful, both of you."

"If we really wanted to be careful we wouldn't get in the water," Watch muttered.

They got in the water anyway. Watch let the air out of Adam's BC—his buoyancy control device, whatever that was. Almost immediately Adam began to sink. Yet he didn't panic. He had never been underwater with a mask on before, and he was amazed at how beautiful it was. Different colored fish swam by. The sunlight shining through the surface of the water was like a ray from an alien sun.

They sank steadily and didn't stop until they were down thirty feet. Adam could at least read his depth gauge. Unfortunately, it was much darker than it had been near the surface. Adam could only see ten feet in any direction. Watch bobbled beside him and raised a hand in an okay gesture. Adam flashed back an okay sign.

Watch had been right about one thing. Adam felt completely weightless, as if he were in outer space. It was a great feeling. He was glad he had decided to give it a try.

Watch pointed out toward deeper water, away from the jetty and over to the reef. He wanted Adam to follow. Adam nodded his head. It was interesting communicating without talking.

They moved forward. Adam quickly discovered that he swam faster if he didn't use his arms, just his fins. He felt very comfortable under the water, and his fear of sharks almost went away. He watched as his silver bubbles rose slowly to the surface. He wondered if Cindy and Sally could see their bubbles.

Two minutes later they were at the reef. They were now forty-five feet down, and it was as dark as half an hour after sunset. The reef was not made of coral, but of jagged rock. Watch had explained that coral only grew in warm water. As they drifted over it, searching for signs of a wrecked ship, Adam imagined he was floating over the surface of a distant moon. Even though it was dark, up close the beautiful colors remained. He wished he had a camera to take pictures to show his family. He knew they wouldn't believe his story without proof. He wouldn't have believed it himself.

Watch handed Adam a flashlight. Adam didn't know why he hadn't given it to him on the surface, but figured Watch must have been afraid he would lose it before he grew comfortable underwater. The flashlights were small, not very powerful, but the beams lit up the rocks somewhat. Watch flashed his light in and out of the crevasses for any sign of the wreck.

They had been searching the reef for maybe thirty minutes when Adam suddenly felt something slide down his front. Looking down, he realized Watch had not tightened his weight belt enough. It was about to slip off. The weights, Adam knew, helped hold him down. He had not forgotten his lungs would explode if he rushed to the surface. A wave of terror swept over him. Instead of grabbing the slipping belt, he grabbed Watch's arm and pointed frantically at what was happening.

Watch looked over.

At that moment Adam's weight belt fell off completely.

The belt sank like a rock, disappearing into a deep crevasse.

Adam felt himself begin to float upward. Quickly.

Oh no, Adam thought. His lungs would explode.

Soon he would see his blood. *Yuck.*

He would die. The fish would have him for food.

But Watch grabbed him and pulled him down hard, shaking his head. Adam didn't need the lecture. He knew he was supposed to go up slowly. But without the weights, it seemed impossible to stay down. But drag him down Watch did, until they were floating beside the top of the reef. Watch reached over, grabbed a rock, and stuffed it in one of the pockets on Adam's BC. Immediately Adam sank down, and Watch was able to let him go. Watch pointed to the place where the weight belt had disappeared and then pointed to himself. He was going to search for the belt. Adam was to wait for him. Adam nodded vigorously.

Watch disappeared.

Adam sat on the edge of the reef and wondered if it was logical to be searching for a ghost in shark-infested waters. With Watch gone, it was hard to stop thinking about sharks. He had heard that great whites could weigh more than three thousand pounds. The shark could have Adam for a snack and still be hungry.

He wished Watch would hurry and get back with his weight belt.

But Watch didn't come back.

Ten minutes went by. Fifteen.

Still no Watch.

Adam checked his air gauge: 500 psi. He assumed that meant he was almost out of air. He had to start back soon, but how could he without Watch? Sally would yell at him and call him a chicken again. Besides, he liked Watch and didn't think his friend would leave him alone on purpose.

Adam's air gauge sank to 400 psi, then 300 psi.

He would need what little air he had left to make it back to the surface.

Maybe a shark got Watch.

Adam groaned behind his face mask, unsure of what to do.

It was then that he saw the wreck.

At first he wasn't sure what it was. Just a glimmer of white in the eerie blue-black. It was off to his left, almost behind him, which was why he hadn't seen it earlier. But it didn't look that far away; it couldn't be if he was able to see it at all. He wondered if Watch had seen it on the way back from retrieving the weight belt. Maybe Watch was already inside the wreck,

Adam thought. That would explain why he hadn't returned.

Adam made a decision. He would check out the boat for one minute, no more. Then he had to head back up, with or without Watch.

Adam swam slowly toward the wreck.

It grew in size. The boat had been a motor yacht maybe sixty feet long. Adam could see the gash in the front where the hull had hit the rocks. He had to assume that farther out the rocks were closer to the surface. He could even read the faint lettering on the side. Thirty years had not washed it away. He was definitely looking at the *Halifax*.

Adam checked his air: 200 psi.

He had to return to the surface. Now.

But just as he turned to swim up, he thought he saw several small bubbles float out of the hole in the hull. The opening was three feet across. He wondered if Watch had swum inside and become stuck. If that was true, Watch's air would be running out.

Adam made another hard decision.

He would swim into the hole.

Just a quick look around and then back out.

But Adam had to dive down slightly to reach the hole. He was now fifty-five feet underwater, and he vaguely remembered Watch saying he had to stop for three minutes at fifteen feet before going to the surface. Well, Adam thought, that was one stop he wouldn't have time to make. Maybe his lungs would explode after all. Yet he wasn't as scared as he had been earlier. He had to save his friend. He was doing what he had to do.

Adam swam into the crack in the hull.

His flashlight was out in front of him. He swam into the bow of the boat, into a storage room of some kind. He disturbed a mop and pail, and they floated up. The walls closed around him and it seemed that his light dimmed. He hoped Watch had checked the batteries before they went under. He hoped he found Watch soon. The storage room was partially crushed, and the way was narrow. Adam imagined how easy it would be to get stuck inside, without being able to turn around.

Something jumped out at him.

It had sharp teeth. Big eyes. An ugly face.

Adam screamed inside his mask.

He dropped his flashlight.

Everything went dark. Perfectly black.

Oh-no. Oh-no. Oh-no.

At that moment Adam knew he was doomed. The horrible creature coming toward him was about to take a big bite out of his face, and then it would crawl through the hole and eat his brains. For several terrifying seconds Adam floated frozen, waiting to be devoured by the monster from the deep.

Yet the seconds ticked by and nothing bit him. Also, when he finally opened his eyes, he realized that his flashlight had not gone out. It was floating just below his feet. Only the beam was pointing into a closet and was no longer lighting up the storage area. It had gone black because he had almost blacked out.

Adam reached down and grabbed his light.

He saw the creature again.

And screamed again.

Then he stopped, embarrassed.

The creature looked scary, but it wasn't that big. He realized he was looking at a one-foot-long electric eel, which was similar to an underwater snake. The little eel actually seemed more terrified of him. Adam flicked his hand once, and the thing darted away. Now Adam decided it was time for him to get away. If Watch had entered the wreck, he wasn't there now.

Adam turned and swam back the way he'd come.

He thought he was going back the way he'd come.

But he didn't emerge back into the ocean.

Instead, he found himself in a stateroom.

He floated up into it and shone his light around.

He must have gotten turned around.

Probably when he closed his eyes and screamed into his mask.

Adam noticed something funny about the large stateroom. It was filled with air. It was a good thing. Adam checked his own air supply. Again he almost fainted. His panic attack with the electric eel had drained his tank.

He had 0 psi.

Adam gagged on the regulator in his mouth.

It was not giving him any more air.

He pulled it out of his mouth and drew in a deep breath. The air in the stateroom was old and smelled like fish. But at least it fed his lungs; he wasn't about to complain. Adam couldn't believe how he had gotten himself into such a mess. He was fifty-five feet underwater and his tank was completely empty. Worse, no one knew where he was.

Adam searched around some more with his flashlight.

It was then that he saw something worse than an electric eel.

A million times worse.

It was a slimy skull. A whole skeleton.

It floated toward him.

Adam screamed. No one heard him.

And the skeleton kept coming.

7

"I LOST HIM," WATCH SAID AS HE CLIMBED back onto the jetty.

"What?" Sally screamed. "How could you lose him?"

Watch sat on a boulder and pulled his face mask off. "He dropped his weight belt and I went down to retrieve it. But it was stuck between two rocks. I had a hard time getting it loose. When I finally returned to where I'd left Adam, he wasn't there." Watch glanced around. "I don't suppose either of you has seen him?"

"Of course we haven't seen him!" Sally yelled. "You were supposed to take care of him!"

"I'm sorry," Watch said.

"You're sorry!" Sally cried. "You just murdered my future senior prom date!"

"It's a long time till senior year," Watch said. "You might meet someone else you like."

Cindy had tears in her eyes. "Is Adam really dead?" she asked.

Watch hung his head sadly. "I'm completely out of air. He has to be, too. Unless he grew gills in the last few minutes, I don't see how he can be alive." Watch looked out to sea and sighed. "He was so young."

Cindy put her hand to her head. "Oh no. This is all my fault. Poor Adam."

"Stop sobbing," Sally snapped at Cindy. "It ain't over till it's over." Sally paused to think. "Why would Adam have left the spot where you left him? We have to ask ourselves this question."

Watch shrugged. "Maybe a shark got him."

Cindy wept louder.

"Would you please quit being so depressing!" Sally yelled.

"But you're the one who's been talking about sharks all day," Watch said.

"That was before Adam was missing." Sally froze suddenly and then snapped her fingers. "I got it! Adam left the spot where you last saw him because he saw the wreck. It's the only explanation."

"I didn't see the wreck," Watch said, rubbing the water off his thick glasses, which he had worn under his custom-made mask.

"Yeah, but you're half blind," Sally said, pacing. "This is logical. And if Adam did go inside the wreck, there's a good chance he found an air pocket. He could still be alive. We have to get more air. We have to go back down for him."

"We?" Watch asked.

"Yes," Sally said proudly. "I will risk my life to save Adam because my love for him is more powerful than my fear of death." She stopped and glared at crying Cindy. "I bet you can't say the same thing."

Cindy wiped at her face. "I don't mind going after him."

Watch nodded. "You two go while I rest."

Sally threw another tantrum. "You have to go because you're the only one who knows where you left him! You have to go back to that spot and search for the wreck. It has to be in that area." Sally paused. "Actually, you'll have to go alone. We don't have any more scuba equipment."

"So much for your brave promise to save Adam," Cindy said.

Sally sneered. "It's the thought that counts. But you can rest for a few minutes, Watch, while Cindy and I get you another air tank. Come on, Cindy, and quit sassing me. Adam's life is all that matters now."

Watch nodded. "I'll stay here to see if any huge trails of blood float to the surface."

Sally shook her head as she walked away. "Somehow I get the feeling you don't know what a positive attitude means," she said.

8

ADAM HAD STOPPED SCREAMING. THE REA-
son the skeleton had been rushing toward him was
because—in his panic—he had been splashing in the
water and created a mild current inside the stateroom.
This had set the skeleton free to float toward him. The
skeleton was not alive, after all, but as dead as any other
creature that had gone down with the ship. Too bad
Mr. Spiney wasn't around to inspect it, Adam thought.
The librarian probably would have loved the old sailor's
strong white bones.

Adam didn't know if anyone was coming to his rescue. He hoped someone was because he didn't like to
think what his bones would look like after he'd been

rotting in the ship for a few years. He didn't know what he could do to help his friends locate him. He wished Watch had given him a flare gun along with the flashlight. One thing was sure, he knew he couldn't swim to the surface without another tank of air. He'd just have to be patient.

While waiting, Adam studied the contents of the stateroom, trying to get an idea of what Captain Pillar had been like. Just looking at his skeleton didn't tell Adam much. There were the usual things one would expect to be floating about: books, chairs, boxes of food, and cans of soup. But the most dominant item in the yacht was booze. It seemed that Captain Pillar had gone to sea with gallons of alcohol. Indeed, when Adam examined the skeleton closer he saw that Captain Pillar had plunged to his watery grave tightly clutching a bottle of whiskey. Even in death, he couldn't give up the stuff.

It made Adam wonder if the broken lighthouse had had anything to do with the wreck of the ship. Adam was pretty sure Captain Pillar had been so drunk that dark night thirty years ago that he hadn't known where he was going, searchlight or no searchlight. If Captain Pillar's ghost had swiped Neil, it had no right to do it.

But Adam was almost positive there was no Neil

down here. And he had a feeling that there never had been. Sally had jumped to her conclusion too fast. Adam doubted that Captain Pillar had anything to do with the disappearance of the boy. At least not directly.

Adam just hoped he lived to tell his friends about his important observations.

Time went by, and Adam began to get cold. He had on a wet suit, of course, but it didn't keep him nearly so warm now that he'd stopped swimming. But he couldn't move around too much because he'd use up the air quicker.

He had another problem. The battery in his flashlight was dying. Every minute or so, the light would briefly flicker out. Each time it came back on, it was slightly dimmer. The underwater boat was spooky enough with light. In the dark, Adam didn't know if he'd be able to stand it. The cold would seep into his heart and lungs, and he wouldn't even be able to shout for help. He reconsidered. Maybe he should try to make one last dash for the surface. If his lungs exploded, at least it would be over for him soon.

But Adam stayed where he was.

He didn't want his lungs to explode.

He was sure it would hurt real bad.

More time passed. His light flickered.

But this time it didn't come back on.

"Oh no," Adam whispered as he shook the flashlight. He played with the switch, turning it on and off. But it remained off.

He was alone, in the dark. Underwater with a dead sailor.

"This is worse than the Secret Path," Adam whispered as he began to shiver. He'd never been in such a cold black place. He tried to think back to how it had all got started. Really, he'd just wanted his big excitement that day to be doughnuts and milk.

"Yeah, but you wanted to be the big hero, too," he told himself. That was the trouble with most movies and books, he decided. They didn't tell the stories of all the heroes who didn't live to tell their tales. He doubted there would even be an article in *The Daily Disaster* to describe his brave attempt to save Neil.

"It's a stupid name for a paper anyway," Adam said between trembling teeth.

More time went by. Adam began to lose the feeling in his hands, his feet. His constant shivering was slowly being replaced by a strange drowsy warm feeling. He knew that was a bad sign. He was getting hypothermia—he had read about it in one of his mother's magazines. He would pass out soon, and drown, and the fish would eat him. It was a cruel world. It was a weird town.

Then he saw a strange yellow light. He wondered if that meant he was dead, that an angel was coming to take him to heaven. He thought he deserved to go there since he had died so bravely. The light was coming up beneath him and it was getting so very bright. He wondered if his guardian angel would be fat and naked like the ones in the old paintings. He sort of hoped he had a nicer-looking angel, not that he was picky.

But it wasn't an angel.

A human head popped up out of the water.

"Watch," Adam said softly. "What are you doing here?"

Watch took out his regulator and pulled off his face mask. "I've come to rescue you."

"You took long enough," Adam said, although he was happy to see his friend.

"Sorry. I sent the girls for another air tank but they brought back a huge bottle of laughing gas instead. The dive shop in Spooksville also supplies the local dentists. They often get their inventory mixed up. I had to go back to the shop myself." Watch searched around with his flashlight and nodded in the direction of Captain Pillar's skeleton, which was still holding on to its whiskey bottle. "Is that the guy whose ghost stole Neil?" Watch asked.

"I don't think so," Adam replied. "I really think the ghost is up in the lighthouse. I think there's only one ghost. Remember that howling we heard? And there was no way that searchlight could have come on by itself."

Adam went on to explain his theory that the boat had crashed because the captain had been drunk, not because the searchlight was off. Watch thought that made sense. But he wanted to bring the skeleton with them anyway.

"Why?" Adam asked.

"Because you never know," Watch said. "The ghost in the lighthouse might want to talk to it."

Adam snickered. "Skeletons can't talk."

"Yeah, and ghosts aren't supposed to exist. Don't forget where you're living. I wouldn't be surprised if the skeleton and the ghost got in a big argument. It won't be the first time that's happened around here."

Adam yawned. "We can take it with us if you want. If nothing else, we can give it to Mr. Spiney." He pointed to Watch's air tank. "Did you bring me an extra tank?"

"No. But you don't need it. We can buddy breathe."

"Is that dangerous?" Adam asked.

"Not if just two people are doing it together." Watch glanced again at the skeleton. "I don't think he needs any air."

9

SALLY AND CINDY WERE OVERJOYED TO SEE Adam alive. Adam was surprised at how glad they were. They both had tears in their eyes as he climbed onto the rocks, although Sally quickly brushed hers away. Adam felt pleased to know he would have been missed if he'd died. This hero business did have its rewards. Not that he wanted another kiss or anything gross like that.

"If it wasn't for me, you would still be down there with the fish," Sally said. "I was the one who figured out where you were. I never lost hope, even as Cindy and Watch were planning your funeral."

"That's not true," Cindy said. "In my heart I knew Adam would pull through."

"Yeah, that's why you picked out a tank of laughing gas instead of air," Sally said.

Cindy was insulted. "You chose a tank with a skull and crossbones on it."

"Speaking of bones," Watch said, with Captain Pillar in tow. "This is what Adam found in the ship. Don't worry, Cindy, it's not your brother."

"I can see that," Cindy said, looking a little sick. The skeleton was draped with seaweed, and there was a tiny crab crawling out of one of its eye sockets. "There was no sign of my brother?" Cindy asked quietly.

"No," Adam said. "But I think we've been chasing after the wrong ghost. We have to search the lighthouse again."

"But we already searched it," Sally protested. "Neil wasn't inside. I would—"

"Bet my reputation on it," Watch finished for her.

"We hardly searched the place before leaving," Adam said. "What if the top floor had an attic above it?"

Watch nodded as he stared up at the top of the lighthouse. "There could be a tiny room above the searchlight. At least it looks that way from here." Watch shivered. "But it's getting late and I'm hungry. Maybe we should try to save Neil tomorrow, after a warm meal and a good night's sleep."

Cindy was agitated. "But you really think my brother might be stuck in there with an evil ghost?" she asked Adam. "If it's true, I can't leave him there another night."

"For all we know the ghost might be enjoyable company," Watch said. "Remember Casper. He wasn't a bad fellow."

"He was a whiner," Sally disagreed. "He was always complaining about being dead. He should have had to live in Spooksville for a few weeks, see what we go through. Then he would have stopped his moaning."

Adam shook his head. "We have to go back inside the lighthouse and we have to go now. Before it gets completely dark."

"Should we bring the skeleton?" Watch asked.

"It might look nice hung up beside the spider webs," Sally said.

"I don't care if you bring it," Adam said. "Just get this scuba equipment off my back."

The girls crossed over to the lighthouse on the rope. Watch and Adam were still in their trunks and they swam. This time they had a flashlight. It was good because the sun had set while Adam was trapped underwater. Just as they stepped inside the lighthouse, Sally reminded them that all the bad things that had occurred had happened at this exact time of day.

"You don't have to wait till midnight to see a ghost in this town," Sally said.

Adam was relieved to get inside. The interior of the lighthouse was much warmer than the jetty, and he was able to stop shivering. But it was more than comfort that encouraged him. Adam felt as if they were finally closing in on Neil. What had happened in the lighthouse earlier had scared them. That was why they hadn't come back right away. But after his terror below the sea, Adam felt ready to face anything.

They started up the long spiral staircase. Like the last time, it was hard climbing. Soon they were hot and sweating. But no one asked to stop and rest. Watch continued to drag the skeleton with him. Remarkably, the dead captain still managed to have a hold of his whiskey bottle.

After about ten minutes they reached the trapdoor that led into the upper level. Watch raised his hand for them to stop.

"Now remember," Watch said, "if the searchlight suddenly comes on, close your eyes. We don't want you to stumble around. You might fall down this opening."

"I won't do that again," Cindy said, anxious to keep going.

They entered the upper level. Watch set the

skeleton down and studied the wires on the search-light again. The rest of them examined the wooden ceiling, something they hadn't thought to do before. Adam focused the flashlight on several grooved lines in the wood.

"Those look like they could be the outline of a door of some kind," Adam said, pointing.

"But how are we going to get up there?" Sally asked. "And how are we going to open the door? There's no knob, no lock."

"Let me go up first and check it out," Adam said. He tapped Watch on the shoulder. "Help me shove that desk over, and then I'll put that chair on top of it."

Watch studied the ceiling. "You still won't be able to reach it."

"I will if I stand on your shoulders," Adam said.

Watch was impressed. "If you fall, you'll break your neck." He added, "You might pull me down with you."

"It's a risk we'll have to take," Adam said firmly.

"There he goes trying to impress Cindy again," Sally muttered.

"I'll follow you up into the attic, Adam," Cindy said, interrupting Sally with a nasty look.

Together they moved the desk. Watch and Adam climbed onto the desk, and Sally and Cindy handed them the chair. Watch carefully positioned the chair and got up on it, taking a moment to balance himself.

"How much do you weigh?" Watch asked Adam.

Adam shrugged. "I don't know. Less than you."

"If you fall, don't grab my hair," Watch said. "And tuck the flashlight in your belt. But keep it on."

Adam did as he was told. Then he looked back up at Watch. "How am I supposed to get up on your shoulders?" he asked.

"It's your plan," Sally muttered.

"Climb up on the chair beside me," Watch said. Again, Adam did what he was told. "Good. Now give me your foot. I'll boost you up. Remember what I said about my hair."

"If I lose my balance, can I at least grab your ears?" Adam asked.

"I suppose," Watch said. "Just don't pull too hard. I don't want to have to go to the hospital to have them sewn back on."

"Spooksville's main hospital is located only a block from the cemetery," Sally said. "And there's a good reason. There's a surgeon who works there who has this thing about people's spare parts. Every time he operates, he tries to get out all the spare parts. I know this kid at school, Craig, who went into the hospital to have his tonsils out. And this surgeon removed one of Craig's lungs while he was at it. Now we all call Craig *Breathless.*" Sally added, "But at least he doesn't have to take PE anymore."

"What's this surgeon's name?" Adam asked, thinking if he ever got sick he'd be sure his parents didn't request him.

"Dr. Jonathan Smith," Sally said. "But the hospital staff just calls him *Dr. Ripper.*"

"Could we please have a little less history," Cindy said. "And a little more action."

Sally was insulted. "You haven't lived here long. At times like this, a little knowledge of Spooksville might save your life. Why I remember one time this troll was—"

"I'm going up," Adam interrupted. "Ready, Watch?"

Watch clasped his hands together for Adam to step on. "Ready. The second you step on my shoulders, brace your arm on the ceiling. That should keep you from falling."

Adam hesitated. "You don't have to sneeze or anything?"

"No."

"Good." Adam set his foot in Watch's cupped hands, and Watch boosted him up. With his other foot Adam immediately stepped up and onto Watch's shoulder. For an instant he wobbled dangerously, and he was sure he was going to fall. The floor suddenly seemed so far away. It would be weird to almost drown and then fall to your death in the same day, Adam thought.

"Grab the ceiling!" Watch shouted.

Adam threw his right hand up and touched the ceiling. Actually, there was nothing to grab because the wood was relatively smooth. But, as Watch had said, he was able to brace himself by pressing against the ceiling. In a moment he had regained his balance.

Adam panted. "That was close."

"You weigh a lot more than most twelve-year-olds," Watch grumbled.

"I'm not that big," Adam said.

"You have high density," Watch replied. "I can't hold you long. Study the grooves. Look for a way in."

Adam didn't have to study anything. The moment he touched the space between the grooves, a three-foot-wide panel pushed up into the ceiling. Grabbing the edge with one hand, Adam carefully reached for his flashlight with the other and focused it into the opening.

"Do you see anything?" Cindy asked, anxiously.

"Darkness," Adam said honestly. "I'll have to climb up into the space."

"Be careful," Cindy whispered.

"The time for care has passed," Sally said ominously.

Adam tucked the flashlight back into his belt to keep both hands free. Telling Watch to be extra still, he moved his hands so that he was grabbing the corner of the opening. Counting to three, he yanked up hard with his arms, pulling his body off Watch's shoulders. But he wasn't able to throw his legs into the opening. Suddenly he was dangling in midair, without support. Watch had climbed down from the chair onto the desktop.

"Why did you leave me?" Adam gasped, barely holding on.

"I was afraid you'd kick me in the head," Watch said.

"Don't let go," Cindy called anxiously.

"That's good advice," Sally said sarcastically.

Adam realized that he couldn't hang there all night. His arms were tiring quickly. Taking a deep breath, he tried pulling himself up again. This time he managed to catch the other corner of the opening with one foot. That was all the leverage he needed. A moment later he was sitting on the floor of the dark attic. There were no windows, and no light from the moon or stars got through. The others gathered below him.

"Is my brother there?" Cindy called up.

"Just let me have a look around," Adam said, moving the beam of the flashlight across the room. He had hardly begun to search when a glimpse of a hideous skeleton sitting in a rocking chair jumped out at him. Adam was so startled that he let out a cry and dropped the flashlight.

"Ahhh!" he shouted.

In fact, he dropped the flashlight through the opening in the ceiling.

Luckily, Watch caught it.

"Do you see something interesting?" Sally asked casually.

Adam hugged the edges of the opening and frantically listened for the approach of the skeleton. From his experience on the Secret Path, he knew there were dead people—the good ones—who stayed dead, and dead people—the bad ones—who liked to play with the living. But it was hard to hear anything because his heart was pounding so loud and he was choking on the last breath he had taken.

"What's happening?" Cindy shouted, worried.

"There's a dead person up here," Adam croaked.

"Is that all?" Sally said.

"Is this dead person trying to kill you?" Watch asked matter-of-factly.

"I don't know." Adam gasped. He would have leaped

back down to the desk if he hadn't been sure he would break his neck. He continued to hug the edges of the opening, waiting for a bony hand to settle on his shoulder and rip open his flesh. But after a minute or so into his latest nervous breakdown, nothing happened. Adam finally began to breathe easier. The skeleton wasn't moving.

"Are you under attack?" Sally asked.

"I'm fine," Adam said finally.

"He's fine," Sally said to the others. "He's scared out of his pants, but he's fine."

"Can you throw the flashlight up to me?" Adam asked Watch.

"Sure," Watch said. Carefully, he tossed the flashlight straight up and through the opening. Adam was lucky to catch it on the first try. After a moment's hesitation, Adam focused the light back on the skeleton. She was not a pretty sight, even by a skeleton's standards.

Her hair was long and stringy. It looked like straw that had been dipped in white paint, then left out in the wind to dry. She wore the shreds of a violet dress— that the bugs had been nibbling at for the last thirty years. The wooden chair she sat in looked as if it was about to collapse.

But the most scary thing was her face, or what was left of it. Her jaw hung open. Her few remaining teeth were cracked and gray and yellow. The empty sockets of her eyes glared at him. The darkness inside them seemed particularly deep and cold. Adam had to force himself not to stare. He almost felt as if he were being hypnotized.

Adam realized he was looking at Evelyn Maey.

Last caretaker of Spooksville's lighthouse. Mother of lost Rick.

"Is my brother there?" Cindy asked again.

"I don't see him," Adam replied. "But—"

"But what?" Sally asked when Adam didn't finish his sentence.

Adam cocked his head to the side. "I think I hear something."

"What?" they all asked at the same time.

"I'm not sure," Adam said. The sound was faint, but not far. It was not a howling noise, but something that was equally disturbing. If it belonged to a hungry monster.

Adam thought he heard footsteps. But only for a moment.

He played the light over the attic space.

Nothing beside Mrs. Maey. The sound was gone.

"What's happening?" Sally demanded.

"Nothing," Adam muttered, puzzled.

"Nothing's happening," Sally told the others. "And yet he's driving us crazy with suspense."

"I want to come up there," Cindy said.

"How much do you weigh?" Watch asked, rubbing his shoulders.

"I don't know if you want to bother, Cindy," Adam said. "There's a pretty ugly skeleton up here."

"Like we have a good-looking one down here," Sally said.

"I have to go up there," Cindy insisted.

Watch sighed. "Just don't pull on any of my parts if you lose your balance."

Watch and Cindy climbed up on the chair, and then Watch boosted her up to the ceiling. Because Adam was able to reach down and help her, Cindy didn't have nearly as much trouble getting into the attic as he had. A moment later she was sitting on the dusty floor beside him. Adam pointed the flashlight at Mrs. Maey. Cindy gasped.

"She's ugly," she whispered.

"Dying can do that to you," Adam remarked as he stood up.

Just then several terrifying things happened at once.

The wooden door that led into the attic fell shut.

Cindy tried to pull it back open.

But it was locked tight.

Down below, beside Sally and Watch, the huge searchlight began to move until it was pointed straight up, toward the ceiling.

"What's happening?" Sally screamed.

The searchlight came on.

The light was blinding. Sally and Watch staggered back, covering their eyes. The light was so powerful it pierced through the fine space between the attic boards. As a result, Adam and Cindy—now cut off from their friends—were also blinded. It was as if a sun had just been born under their feet. He grabbed Cindy and pulled her close.

"The trapdoor won't open!" she cried.

"Did you knock it shut?" Adam yelled back.

Because he had to yell to be heard.

Because suddenly there was a loud howling.

As if the ocean wind were breaking in.

Or a ghost was coming to life.

"No!" Cindy cried. "It shut by itself."

"Watch!" Adam called, dropping once more to his knees, trying to pull up the trapdoor. It was more than stuck. It didn't budge; it could have been nailed shut. "Sally!"

They didn't answer. Or if they did their voices were drowned out by the howling. Yet, as he stood and shielded his eyes to look around, Adam knew it was no wind that was making that sound. The attic dust continued to remain undisturbed. No breeze could come in from the outside. The sound was supernatural in origin. They had found their ghost, and it was probably a mistake that Cindy had said how ugly the skeleton was.

Because the ghost was coming back to life.

Where the blinding rays of the searchlight swept the skeleton, Adam saw a strange form begin to take shape. It appeared to be made of both light and dust, as if it drew to it whatever was handy to make its form. As the noise reached a deafening pitch and the walls of the attic began to shake, both Adam and Cindy saw the ghost of an old lady materialize where the skeleton sat.

The skeleton did not vanish. They could still see it, but through the haze of the old lady ghost. And all of a sudden the skeleton didn't look so scary. Because the ghost that stirred in its place was a thousand times worse. It glared at them with strange violet eyes that flashed cold fire. It raised both its arms, and its wrinkled hands were like claws. The razor-sharp nails that bent from the twisted fingertips made Cindy squeal. She had obviously seen those hands before.

"That's the ghost that stole my brother!" she yelled.

"I'm not surprised." Adam gulped. He put an arm around Cindy and carefully pulled her back, away from the ghost, which had climbed to its feet. For a moment the thing searched the attic. But then its angry eyes settled back on them, and it took a step in their direction. Cindy shook in Adam's arms, and he was not feeling exactly strong himself.

"What do you think it wants," Cindy said, gasping.

"One of us," Adam whispered. "Maybe both."

Just then they heard the cries of a young boy.

The sound came from even farther above them.

The attic had an attic.

"Neil!" Cindy cried. "That's my brother." She let go of Adam and strode toward the ghost, anger in her step. "You old ugly ghost!" she swore at the thing. "You give me back my brother!"

"You might not want to insult it," Adam suggested. "Try saying please."

But Cindy was too furious. Overhead, her brother continued to shout, pounding on the ceiling. It was only then that Adam noticed a ladder pinned to the ceiling. Obviously, it could be used to reach the second attic. If he could get to it. Between him and the ladder stood the ghost, and the thing didn't look in the best of moods. Cindy raised a finger and shook it in the ghost's face.

"You had no right to take him," Cindy said. "He never did anything to you." Cindy paused and shouted at the ceiling. "We're coming, Neil!"

"Try getting around to its other side," Adam whispered loudly.

Cindy glanced over her shoulder. "Why?"

"Just do it," Adam said. "I'll explain later. Keep it distracted."

Cindy nodded and turned back to the ghost, which still looked angry, but unsure of what to do with them. Cindy moved to Adam's right. The ghost followed her. Adam began to move to the left.

"Just let Neil go and I won't file criminal charges," Cindy told the ghost. "We can forget the whole thing, pretend it never happened."

The ghost fixed its attention on Cindy. It even moved as she moved. Adam was able to use the opportunity to jump up and grab one end of the ladder. It folded down smoothly, barely creaking. Adam felt a wave of triumph. If he could get up into the second attic and grab Neil, they could be out of here and home in time for dinner. He pushed one end of the ladder to the floor and started up the steps. There was another trapdoor above with a metal catch. He'd have no trouble opening it.

Adam almost made it. Another couple of steps and he'd have reached Neil. But the ghost was not blind.

Adam felt a strong hard hand grip his ankle.

He glanced down, not really wanting to see what had a hold of him.

The ghost glared up at him. Fire burned in its violet eyes as it growled. The other hand wrapped around his other ankle. Then he was falling. The ghost had pulled his feet out from under him.

Adam hit the floor hard. Pain flared through his right side, and he had trouble drawing in a breath. Before he could recover, the ghost was on him. It was awfully strong for an old woman, especially one that had been dead thirty years.

It grabbed him by the arms and lifted him right off the floor. For a moment Adam stared directly into its face. He could still see through it, but it seemed with each passing second the ghost was becoming more solid. It actually had bad breath. It gloated over him and then threw its head back, opening its mouth wide. The howling again shook the attic.

"Maybe we could discuss this," Adam said. "Work out some kind of trade."

The ghost was not in the mood to talk. It carried Adam to the wall, and with one stiff kick it broke a hole in the wall. Adam felt the cold air pour in. The ghost gave another kick and a large section of the wall collapsed. The ghost pushed Adam through the opening. Far below him—one hundred feet at least—he saw the waves crashing against jagged boulders. The wind tossed his hair. The ghost was slowly loosening its hold on him. This was it, he thought, he was going to die. No way could he survive such a fall.

"Adam!" Cindy cried.

The ghost dropped him.

10

MEANWHILE SALLY AND WATCH WERE VERY busy themselves. When the searchlight first came on, they both stumbled around half blind, doing exactly what Watch himself had warned them not to do. This time Sally almost stepped into the trapdoor opening and fell. But Watch bumped into her at that moment. They decided to close the trapdoor.

"What's happening?" Sally repeated. "What's that howling sound?"

"I think the ghost has woken up," Watch said, holding a hand up like a visor to block out the light.

They heard shouts above, but couldn't understand what was being said. "We have to rescue Adam!" Sally cried.

"What about Cindy?" Watch asked.

"We can save her as well," Sally said. "Quick, go up on the desk and the chair."

"No." Watch stopped her. "It's obvious the ghost is up there. They must be trapped. If we go up, we'll just get trapped."

"You're a coward," Sally said. "We can't just leave them."

"I'm not saying we should leave them," Watch said. "But I think this is a powerful ghost. It was able to grab Neil all the way at the far end of the jetty. We have to strike at the heart of its power."

"What's that?" Sally asked.

Watch pointed to the blindingly bright light. "This. Every time the ghost appears, the searchlight comes on."

"You're right!" Sally exclaimed. "Let's bust the bulbs."

It sounded simple enough. The problem was that when Watch lifted the chair to smash the searchlight, he couldn't get near it. The chair struck the beam of light as if it were striking a forcefield. The wood shattered in his hands and splinters went flying everywhere. Watch staggered back and would have fallen if Sally hadn't grabbed him.

"I think the searchlight is haunted as well," Sally said.

Watch straightened up and nodded. "But I still think

we can disable it. Remember Adam said there were cans of kerosene in the storage room downstairs? I didn't have a chance to look, but I think this light is powered by a generator inside the lighthouse. Maybe in that very storage room. The generator probably runs on kerosene. The wiring from it must come straight up under the floor. I know for a fact the old city wiring is not giving this thing any juice. The wires are too worn out."

"What are you going to do?" Sally asked.

"I want to run downstairs and wreck the generator. I hope that'll turn off the searchlight, and shut up the ghost."

"That's great," Sally said. "But what am I supposed to do?"

Watch glanced up at the ceiling. There was so much noise up there; it didn't sound like Adam and Cindy were having an easy time with the ghost.

"Maybe there's something you can do to slow the ghost down until I get to the generator," he said.

"Tell me!" Sally demanded.

"I've been thinking about that article we read in the library. It listed the caretaker's name as Evelyn Maey. And we know her son's name was Rick."

"So?"

"You know the staff at *The Daily Disaster.* They always

217

mess up the facts a little. What if they accidentally left off the letter *k*. What if their last name was really Makey."

Sally blinked. "Like in Cindy Makey?"

"Yes. When we were getting the scuba equipment, Cindy told me her father's name was Frederick, but her mother just called him Fred. But what if her father's *mother* had called him Rick?"

Wonder dawned on Sally's face. "Are you saying that Cindy's father might have been the boy who washed out to sea thirty years ago?"

"Yes. Notice where Cindy lives now. In her father's house, which is right next to the lighthouse."

"That's right! Cindy must be the granddaughter of the ghost! Watch, you're a genius!"

"I've known that since I was four years old."

"Wait a second," Sally said. "The paper said the boy, Rick, was never found."

"And Cindy said her father was raised an orphan. The guy probably washed out to sea and didn't wash up again until he was halfway to San Francisco. It's no surprise he never made it back home."

"And Mrs. Makey died without knowing her son was alive," Sally said, nodding to herself. "That's what's made her such a bitter old ghost."

"That and living here, I think," Watch said.

Sally had one last doubt. "But Frederick must have come back to Spooksville as an adult to claim his mother's house. He must have known where it was."

"Maybe the memory of Spooksville only came back to him as he got older," Watch said.

Sally nodded. "Maybe his foster parents were nicer than that old bag upstairs. He probably didn't want to come home."

"Spooksville's a hard town to come home to," Watch agreed.

They heard a big thump above them.

It sounded like a body had hit the floor.

"You get to the generator," Sally said to Watch. "I'll deal with the ghost."

Watch hurried down the stairs. Sally searched for another entrance to the attic. Outside, beyond the windows through which the searchlight normally shone, was a wooden balcony. Sally had noticed it earlier, from the outside, but had forgotten about it in all the excitement. She wondered if she could climb up onto the rails of the balcony and enter the attic from there. It was worth a try, she decided.

Grabbing the chair, Sally smashed it against the windows. All the glass let go at once, and she was able to step outside onto the balcony without scratching herself. It was only then that she saw a doorway leading to the balcony. She hadn't needed to break the windows, after all. *Oh, well*, she thought. Cindy could pay for the damage.

Sally was out on the balcony studying the guard to see if it could support her weight when plaster and wood started raining down on her and she heard the wall above her being punched through. Turning, she was surprised to see Adam fly through the hole in the lighthouse and sail over the side.

Sally reached out and miraculously caught one of his arms. Adam hung over the side of the balcony, his feet dangling one hundred feet above the rocks.

"Adam!" she screamed, straining to hang on. "What are you doing?"

He looked up at her, his eyes wide as saucers.

"I thought I was about to die." He gasped. "Pull me up. Quick."

"I'm trying! You're so heavy."

"It's my high density, I know."

Somehow, Sally managed to pull Adam up far enough so he could place a foot on the floor of the balcony. From there he had no trouble climbing over the railing. Adam took a moment to catch his breath and get his bearings. During that time, Sally explained Watch's theory about Cindy's being related to the ghost. Actually, Sally took credit for making the connection. The news intrigued Adam. Sally also told him what Watch was up to. Adam nodded toward the hole in the lighthouse wall. The same hole the ghost had just thrown him out.

"We have to get back up inside there," he said. "The ghost will try to kill Cindy next."

"Cindy's a strong girl. She can take care of herself."

"Sally!"

"I was just kidding. Did you see any sign of Neil?"

"Yeah. He's in an attic above the attic. But help me balance on this railing. We don't have time to talk."

Sally steadied Adam as he climbed onto the railing. From there he had no trouble reaching the hole. The only problem was that Sally wasn't able to follow him. She had no one to help her balance on the railing.

"You'll have to talk to the ghost yourself," she called to Adam as he disappeared through the hole. She stayed where she was, however, half expecting Adam to come flying out of the hole again. He was such a dynamic young man.

Inside the attic, Adam was met with a terrifying sight. The ghost had a hold of Cindy and was trying to drag her up the ladder to the second attic, probably to lock her inside with her brother. But Cindy was fighting back hard. She had a handful of the ghost's hair in her hand, and she was yanking on it, which the ghost obviously didn't like. Now the howling became bitter with pain and anger. Adam had to shout over it to be heard.

"Mrs. Makey!" he yelled. "You're holding Cindy Makey, your granddaughter!"

The ghost stopped and glanced over at him. So did Cindy.

"I'm not related to this ugly creature," Cindy swore.

Adam stepped forward. "What was your father's name?"

"I told you," Cindy said. "Frederick Makey. Why?"

Adam came even closer and spoke to the ghost. "What was the name of your son, Mrs. Makey?"

The ghost let go of Cindy and froze, staring at Adam. The fire in its eyes seemed to dim, and suddenly its face didn't look so scary. The light around it softened and took on a warmer yellow glow. The howling stopped as Adam spoke gently.

"Your son's name was Frederick Makey," he answered for the ghost. "The ghost of the ship that sank out on the reef did not steal your son. We have his skeleton below and you can talk to it if you like. He crashed his ship because he was drunk. Not because your light was off. It seems Rick just got washed out to sea. He must have washed ashore far from here, and was unable to get back home. But we know he didn't die that night thirty years ago because he later got married and had a family." Adam paused. "Honestly, Mrs. Makey, Cindy's your granddaughter."

The ghost turned back to Cindy. Gently it reached out to touch her hair. But doubt crossed its face and it stopped. Adam knew he had to act fast.

"Cindy," he said. "Tell Mrs. Makey something only your father and she could have known."

"I don't understand," Cindy mumbled, still standing on the stairs with the ghost only a foot away.

"It could be anything his mother taught him," Adam said. "Anything your father later taught you."

Cindy paused. "He taught me this poem. I know he knew it as a kid, but I don't know who taught it to him."

"Just say it," Adam snapped.

Cindy recited the poem quickly.

> The ocean is a lady.
> She is kind to all.
> But if you forget her dark moods.
> Her cold waves, those watery walls.
> Then you are bound to fall.
> Into a cold grave.
> Where the fish will have you for food.

The ocean is a princess.

She is always fair.

But if you dive too deep.

Into the abyss, the octopus's lair.

Then you are bound to despair.

In a cold grave.

Where the sharks will have you for meat.

"It's sort of a lousy poem," Cindy said after she was finished.

"Please quit using the words *lousy* and *ugly* around Mrs. Makey," Adam said. The ghost's face became thoughtful. Adam asked softly, "Mrs. Makey, did you teach your son that poem?"

The ghost nodded slowly, and as it did a single tear ran over its cheek. The tear did not appear to be made of water, however, but of diamond. It glistened in the glow cast by the powerful searchlight.

Once more the ghost turned back to Cindy. Adam understood what it needed to know. So did Cindy. She reached out to touch the ghost's shoulder.

"He was a great man, my father," Cindy whispered. "He had a happy life. He married a wonderful woman, and had us two kids." Then she lowered her head and there were tears on her face as well. "He died a couple of months ago, in a fire." Cindy sobbed. "I'm sorry. I know you miss him. I miss him, too."

The ghost did a remarkable thing right then. It hugged Cindy. No, it did more than that—it comforted her, and Cindy comforted it. For several seconds they cried in each other's arms, although Adam could not hear the ghost's tears.

Then the powerful light that poured through the floor dimmed.

Cindy and the ghost let go of each other.

Adam stepped forward. "Watch has sabotaged the generator. He's cut the power." Adam looked at the ghost. "I'm sorry. I don't know if this will hurt you. Our friend was just trying to save us."

To Adam's surprise, the ghost smiled and shook its head, as if to say that it was all right. Cindy got the same impression.

"I don't think she cares," Cindy said. "I think she wants to move on now." She grabbed the ghost's hands and spoke excitedly. "You can see my father! Your son!"

The ghost's smile widened. For the last time she hugged Cindy and nodded in Adam's direction. Almost as if to say thank you.

Then the searchlight failed and they were plunged into darkness.

At first it seemed completely dark. Then Adam noticed his flashlight lying on the floor. It was still on and he picked it up. After the searchlight the beam appeared feeble.

The ghost was gone.

Cindy quickly climbed the ladder to the top attic.

A moment later she reappeared with a five-year-old boy in her hands.

"Neil!" She was crying.

"Cindy!" her brother kept shouting happily. "Did you kill the ghost?"

"No," Adam said. "We just showed it the way home."

But their adventures were far from over.

All three of them smelled smoke.

Adam ran over to the door in the floor and opened it easily. But what he saw below did not reassure him. Far down, through the first trapdoor that led onto the steps, he saw huge orange flames on the ground floor of the lighthouse. Sally was in the room with the searchlight also looking down to the ground floor. Before Adam could speak, Watch poked his head through the floor at her feet. He had a big grin on his face.

"I was able to destroy the generator," he said.

"What did you do?" Sally screamed at him. "Blow it up?"

"As a matter of fact that is exactly what I did," Watch said, climbing into the room and standing beside Sally. He glanced back down at the flames, which were rapidly moving through the interior of the lighthouse. He lost his smile as he added, "It's too bad this place doesn't have a fire extinguisher."

"But we're trapped!" Sally screamed. "We're going to die!"

"I don't want to burn to death," Cindy whispered beside Adam, fear in her voice.

"We're not going to die," Adam said. "We've come too far for that to happen." He stood and spoke to all of them. "We're going to have to leap off the balcony and into the water."

"You're crazy," Sally said. "A hundred-foot fall will kill us."

"Not necessarily," Watch said. "It is the surface tension of the water that usually kills people when they jump from high places into water. But if that tension can be broken just before we hit the water, we should be all right."

"What does surface tension mean?" Neil asked his sister.

She rubbed his back. "I'll explain it later, after Watch explains it to me."

"Are you saying that if we have something like a

board hit the water just before we do," Adam said, "we should live?"

"Exactly," Watch said. "Come down here. We'll break a few boards off the balcony railing."

Adam first helped Cindy and Neil down the ladder to join Watch and Sally and then climbed down himself. They hurried onto the balcony. A sharp cold wind had come up. It tore at their hair, while far below they could see huge waves crashing on the rocks. The surf had come up in the last few minutes.

It wasn't difficult to tear the railing apart to get all the boards they needed. Soon they each had a couple.

But they were quickly running out of time. Flames burst through to the searchlight room. The bulbs of the light fizzled and then exploded in a gruesome shower of glass and sparks. Orange light bathed the surroundings. The temperature soared.

"Do we throw them over the side ahead of us?" Sally asked.

"No," Watch said. "You'd never catch up with them. Throw the boards below you *after* you jump. They should hit the water a second before you."

"What if I hit to the side of my boards?" Sally asked.

"Then you'll die," Watch said.

There was nothing to say after that. There was no

time to talk anyway. Fire licked out at them on the balcony. Smoke filled the air. It was almost impossible to breathe. They were all coughing. Together they drew back from the opening they had created in the railing. They needed a running start so they could fly beyond the rocks. Cindy held Neil in her arms, and wouldn't part with him, although Adam offered to take the boy. Adam realized he would have to throw Cindy's boards out for her.

They nodded at each other and then ran.

Over the side they flew.

It was the scariest thing imaginable.

For Adam it felt as if he fell forever. The cold wind ripped at his face and hair. He saw the waves, the rocks—all spun together. The ground seemed to take the place of the sky. He wasn't even sure which way was up and which way down. But he remembered to throw out his handful of boards.

Then there was an incredible smash.

Adam felt as if he had been crushed into a pancake.

Everything went cold and black.

He realized he was under the water. He couldn't see the others and for the moment he couldn't worry about them. He swam for the surface, hoping he was going in the right direction. A few seconds later his head broke into the night air. It felt wonderful to draw in a deep breath. He was the first one up. But the others appeared quickly, tiny heads peeking out of the rough surf.

"Can you swim?" he shouted at Neil.

"I'm a great swimmer," the boy said proudly.

They swam to the end of the jetty, where they had earlier tied the rope. They had to time getting onto the rocks, so they didn't get crushed by waves. But the night was finally kind. There was a sudden lull in the waves and soon they were on dry land. Or at least on a bunch of rocks that they could walk on to dry land.

Cindy was so excited to see her brother. She refused to let go of Neil, hugging him and burying him with kisses. Adam was happy for both of them.

"Your mom will be surprised to see your brother again," he told Cindy.

"That's putting it mildly," Cindy said. "Oh, I want you to meet my mother. She likes to meet all the guys I hang out with."

"It's not clear yet whether you and Adam will be having an ongoing relationship," Sally said.

Cindy chuckled. "I think we're all going to be friends. Even you and me, Sally."

"We'll see," Sally said, doubtful. But then she smiled and patted Watch and Adam on the back. "Another heroic mission successfully concluded. I must say you guys did a good job."

"You were the one who figured out the secret of the mystery," Adam said. "Without you, the ghost would have killed us all."

"What's this?" Watch asked.

"Nothing," Sally said quickly. "I'll explain it to you later." She pointed out to sea. "It's amazing we never saw any sharks today. I guess these waters aren't as dangerous as I thought."

But Sally spoke too soon.

A huge white fin sailed by just then.

They jumped up on the biggest rock and grabbed on to one another.

"You must never forget where we live," Adam whispered.

"Ain't that the truth," Sally said, gasping.

On the way home they stopped for doughnuts. Except for Neil, they all ordered coffee. They needed to settle their nerves. The day had been a little too exciting.

THE HAUNTED CAVE

1

Adam Freeman was having ice cream with his friends when the subject of the Haunted Cave came up. The ice-cream parlor was called the Frozen Cow, and it supposedly offered a choice of fifty flavors. They were listed on a large colorful bulletin board that hung behind the counter where the grumpy old man who owned the place stood. But the owner—even when asked politely—refused to give any customer anything but vanilla. Even chocolate and strawberry weren't available. Sally explained that the owner—whom she called Mr. Freeze—was a purist and believed that vanilla was the only ice cream worth serving. Adam had managed to persuade the man to make him a vanilla milkshake.

Of course, since this was Spooksville, Adam had to pay Mr. Freeze double not to use spoiled milk.

"Did you know that monkeys and apes love ice cream?" Watch said, working on a banana split that was made of bananas, vanilla ice cream, and nothing else. "Gorillas like it as well, although I've heard they'll only eat chocolate ice cream."

"They wouldn't like this place," Sally Wilcox muttered, frantically licking a melting ice-cream cone as if it would explode if she lost a drop.

"I thought monkeys and apes were vegetarians," Cindy Makey remarked.

Sally chuckled. "A vegetarian can eat ice cream. You don't kill the cow to get the milk out, you know. You just tug on the udders."

Cindy gave an exaggerated sigh. "I know that. I mean I thought that monkeys and apes *preferred* fruit to dairy products."

Watch shook his head. "That's not so. They're like kids—they'll take ice cream over bananas any day. And as far as I'm concerned, that proves Darwin's theory of natural selection. Man—and woman—evolved from monkeys. We're nothing but talking apes."

"But that's only a theory," Adam protested. "I don't believe it."

"You're reacting to the idea emotionally," Watch said. "It upsets you to think your ancestors used to need a shave twenty-four hours a day. In scientific matters you have to be cold and dispassionate."

"Look who's having the bananas," Sally muttered.

"I'm not reacting emotionally," Adam replied, insulted. "Science has never proven that we evolved from apes. You're forgetting the missing link."

"What about it?" Watch asked.

"It's still missing," Adam said, having a sip of his shake.

"What's the missing link?" Cindy asked.

"A non-vegetarian monkey," Sally said.

"It's a creature that would be half ape, half human," Watch explained. "Adam has a point. Science has never positively found a creature that is directly between us and apes on the evolutionary scale." Watch paused and glanced at Sally. "Of course not many scientists have been to Spooksville."

Sally shook her head vigorously. "Don't start talking about that. We're not going there, no way."

"Going where?" Adam wanted to know, certain he'd missed part of the conversation.

Watch leaned closer and lowered his voice. "The Haunted Cave."

Sally cringed. "Don't say it. To even speak the name will curse us."

"He already said it," Cindy said. "And there's no such thing as a curse."

Sally snorted. "Listen to the girl whose brother was kidnapped by a ghost last week. This whole town is cursed. I know, I was born here."

Cindy smiled. "Yeah, now that you mention it, I guess I can see the damage."

Adam chuckled. "Sally was cursed in the womb."

Sally fumed. "For your information I was born on Friday the thirteenth, which is practically a religious holiday in this town."

"So?" Adam said, puzzled.

"She's saying she wasn't cursed until she was born," Watch explained. "Anyway, this cave is fascinating. There are plenty of stories about creatures inside the cave that could be the missing link."

"Have you ever seen these creatures?" Adam asked skeptically.

"No, but I think a friend of mine did," Watch said. "His name was Bill Balley. He was a camera nut. He went in to photograph them and that was the last we heard of him."

"They found his camera though," Sally said. "It was smeared with blood."

"I think it was peanut butter and jelly," Watch said. "There was film in the camera. I helped develop it. The negatives were in lousy shape but one shot showed a blurry image of a hairy manlike creature."

"How big was the creature?" Adam asked.

"Hard to say," Watch said. "I couldn't tell how far away it had been taken, and there were no reference objects."

"It was big enough to eat Bill," Sally said.

"But I'd guess a missing link should be small," Adam said. "If it's half man, half ape."

"Bill probably thought the same thing," Sally retorted.

"I don't believe any of this," Cindy said.

Sally got mad. "You just moved here a month ago. You don't know anything about this town; therefore, your opinion is totally worthless."

Cindy turned to Adam. "Why don't we go have a look at this cave and prove to these guys there are no missing links running around this town?"

"I believe they run under the town," Watch said.

Adam considered. "We could do that, but I don't think we want to go inside the cave."

"Why not?" Cindy asked.

"Because one of these creatures might eat you alive," Sally said. "Adam knows that, but he's too much under your spell to say it out loud."

"I'm not under nobody's spell," Adam said angrily.

Sally snorted. "You're not under *anyone's* spell. You get so dizzy when you sit next to Cindy you can't even speak right."

"Why are you always yelling at Adam?" Cindy demanded.

"Because I believe he can be helped," Sally explained patiently. "Unlike some people I know."

Cindy stood. "Where is this cave? I want to go there right now. I want to see these creatures—*if* they really exist."

Watch checked one of his four watches. "It's getting late. You might want to explore the cave tomorrow."

"Bill disappeared later in the day," Sally added.

"It makes no difference what time of day we go in the cave," Cindy said. "As long as we have flashlights. Isn't that right, Adam?"

"Right," Adam agreed reluctantly. But even though he had lived in Spooksville for only two weeks, he had seen enough to know there might be something behind Watch's strange story. He didn't want Cindy thinking he was a coward, but he wished they could bring a hunting rifle as well as flashlights. Something powerful enough to stop a large hairy creature.

2

THE HAUNTED CAVE WAS LOCATED NEAR the town reservoir. Up in the hills behind Spooksville. The path to the cave was rugged, so they weren't able to take their bikes. As a result they didn't reach the cave until nearly seven. It was summer and the days were long, but the sun was already close to the horizon.

The opening of the cave didn't look scary. It was just a narrow crack in the rocky hillside that faced the reservoir. The entrance wasn't high—a grown man would have to stoop to get inside. Adam poked his head in and peered around with one of the flashlights they'd picked up at Watch's. All he saw were dirt walls, nothing spectacular.

"I don't see any creatures," he said as he pulled his head back out.

"That's what I call a thorough search," Sally said sarcastically. She pointed to the ground at Adam's feet. "That's where they found Bill's camera. I think they found some of his skin as well."

"That wasn't skin—it was his lunch bag," Watch said. He also peered in the cave, using the other flashlight they had brought. "It goes way back. In fact, I've heard it goes down deep and its tunnels wind around under most of the city."

"Is there another entrance?" Adam asked.

"Not that I know of," Watch said, straightening up.

Cindy appeared anxious to get going. "Well, are we going inside or what?"

Watch shook his head. "I think I'll wait out here for you guys."

"Why?" Adam asked. "You always like a good adventure."

"I think one of us should be here in case you don't come back," Watch said. "I can tell your families not to set places for you at dinner. Stuff like that."

"I can stay," Sally offered quickly. "I don't like caves much anyway."

"Coward," Cindy said.

Sally was instantly furious. "How dare you call me a coward? Why, when you were playing with Barbie and Ken, I was out fighting witches and warlocks."

Cindy was not impressed. "Then why are you afraid to explore the cave with Adam and me?"

Sally wore a mocking smile as she turned to Adam. "Is brave and resourceful Adam ready to explore the cave with dear, spunky Cindy?"

Adam hesitated. Standing near the entrance, he could feel a faint warm breeze coming from inside. He wondered where it came from. The air in most caves was cooler than the outside air. There was also a faint smell to this air. He was reminded of a barbecue, of the odor of dying coals.

"I think we could go in a little way and look around," Adam said finally.

"The creatures are supposed to live way in the back," Watch said. "You won't see anything if you just go in a few feet."

Cindy grabbed Watch's flashlight. "I say we go in all the way. But stay here if you want, Sally. We'll understand if you're too chicken. Adam and I don't need your help."

Sally smoldered. "I dislike being called chicken. Especially by a girl who couldn't rescue her own baby brother from a senile ghost."

Cindy held up a finger to Sally's face. "And who fought hand to hand with the ghost? It was Adam and me."

"And who figured out who the ghost really was?" Sally shot back.

"I did," Watch said.

"Really?" Adam asked. That was news to him.

"Listen," Sally interrupted. "I'm not afraid to explore this cave. I just don't want to get my hair dirty because I washed it this morning."

Cindy snorted. "You're just afraid of having your hair ripped out of your head."

"That is never pleasant," Watch said. "Sally, if you don't want to go inside, that's all right with me. We can sit here and shout words of encouragement if they start screaming."

"That's very noble of you," Adam said.

Sally stood, undecided. "If we do go in, and do see anything that might eat us—anything at all—we get out quick."

Adam nodded. "That sounds reasonable." He checked the flashlight he was carrying. They had picked them up at Watch's house. "Are the batteries fresh?"

"They should last a few hours," Watch said.

Adam nodded. "I'm sure we won't be gone that long."

He ducked inside the cave, Cindy and Sally following at his heels. Adam didn't know it at the time, but he was going to be in the cave much longer than any flashlight would last.

3

THE INTERIOR OF THE CAVE WAS DEFINITELY warmer. Adam noticed the change in temperature the moment he stepped in. The warmth continued to puzzle him. The air currents were definitely blowing out of the cave, not into it. He wondered if there wasn't another entrance nearby.

The size of the cave seemed to expand the moment they were inside. The ceiling was higher than his bedroom ceiling by at least two feet. The walls—six feet apart—were not the simple dirt he had imagined from the outside. Touching them, Adam saw that they were only coated with dust. Actually, the walls were made of hard black rock, which felt smooth beneath Adam's fingers.

Cindy studied the section of wall beside him. "It's like the volcanic rock in Hawaii," she said, carrying the other flashlight.

"You've been to Hawaii?" Sally asked with a huff. "Must be nice."

"We used to go regularly before my father died," Cindy said quietly.

"Are there any geysers around Spooksville?" Adam asked Sally.

"Besides your temper," Cindy added.

"The fountain at the city hall explodes in steam every now and then," Sally said, throwing Cindy a nasty look. "No one knows why."

Adam gestured with his light to a tunnel that ran deeper into the cave. It definitely sloped down, in the direction of the city. "Do you guys notice that faint burning smell?" he asked. "I think there might be hot lava down there."

"That's one good reason to turn back now," Sally muttered.

"I don't know," Cindy said. "The smell and the heat might just be from a hot spring. I want to go deeper."

"Why are you so excited to meet an ape man?" Sally asked.

Cindy shrugged. "If there really are such creatures in here, it would be the discovery of a lifetime."

"If there really are such creatures in here," Sally countered, "your lifetime might be very short."

They moved farther down into the cave. The tunnel became steep, and they had to crouch down to keep from slipping. Soon they were practically on their butts, and their pants were getting dirty. Adam worried that if it got any steeper they'd need a rope to climb out. He was about to suggest they turn back when they heard a faint sound coming from deeper inside the cave. It echoed for several seconds, like an otherworldly lullaby, haunting and hypnotic. It didn't sound like a monster, but it didn't sound human either. The three of them froze.

"What was that?" Cindy whispered.

"It doesn't sound like Bill," Sally whispered back.

"Shh." Adam held up his hand. The sound did not repeat itself, but it sure had their hearts pounding. Adam wiped sweat from his forehead. He had to strain to keep his voice calm. "I think there's something alive down there."

"Like we haven't been saying that all along," Sally said, hissing.

Adam glanced at Cindy, who appeared to be having second thoughts about making important scientific discoveries. "We could come back another time," he suggested. "When we have more time."

"When we're feeling suicidal," Sally added.

Cindy hesitated. "Did we really hear something? Or did we just imagine it?"

"You don't need an imagination in this town," Sally said. "Reality is nightmarish enough. I say let's get out of here before it eats us."

"I honestly do think there's something down there," Adam said to Cindy. He added, "And it doesn't sound like it's in a good mood."

Cindy thought for a moment more, then shrugged. "We can always come back later."

"That's my brave girl," Sally said.

They turned and started back up the slippery floor of the cave. Pushing and pulling on each other, they were able to make it back up to where the floor was relatively flat. By then they were sweating heavily and were anxious to get outside and draw in deep breaths of fresh air.

Adam could see the cave opening thirty feet in front of him. He could even see Watch through the entrance crack—no doubt watching the sun set. Adam was about to call out to him when the girls started fighting again for what seemed the millionth time.

"I never said it sounded like a scary creature," Cindy said. "I would have gone on."

"She says that now that she's running away," Sally said.

"Listen," Cindy snapped. "If anyone's running, it's you. We had to drag you in here in the first place."

Sally stopped and turned on Cindy. "I admit that I don't enjoy being in this cave. You'd have to be a caveman with a low caveman IQ to like it. But you—Ms. Archaeological Overachiever Herself—are bugging the heck out of me pretending to be brave. You're more scared than the rest of us. You're a hypocrite, in other words, and I can't stand hypocrites. They remind me of myself before I overcame my major psychological hangups." She added, "I don't see what Adam sees in you."

"Oh, brother," Adam said.

Cindy got up on her toes. "I bug you? You know that's like a rattlesnake saying to a well-mannered rabbit that the rabbit is annoying it. Just when the snake is about to bite the rabbit."

"I don't have a rattle," Sally snapped.

"Yeah, but you've got a poison tongue," Cindy said. "I wish for just once you would shut up. That you would close your mouth, shut it tight, and forget English and any other language you know for a twenty-four-hour period. Then maybe the rest of us—"

"Stop!" Adam shouted suddenly. He paused to stare

at the opening of the cave. The light from the outside had just flickered slightly.

"What is it?" Sally asked quickly.

Adam pointed to the opening. "Did any of you notice something move over there?"

"No," Cindy said.

"What do you mean?" Sally asked.

Adam frowned. "The entrance looks narrower."

"That's ridiculous," Sally said. Then she froze. "It is narrower!"

Cindy jumped in place. "The opening is closing! Let's get out of here!"

Cindy was right, the entrance was actually closing up. The smooth black rock could have turned molten. It seemed to flow together as they ran toward Watch and the outside. Watch had also noticed the change in the entrance size. But he wasn't foolish enough—or brave enough—to jump inside and try to rescue them. He waved to them, however, to hurry. Unfortunately, the second they reached the entrance, the edges pushed in closer, and the space looked too tight to squeeze through. Adam and Cindy and Sally looked at one another desperately. They were each thinking the same thing. If they tried to squeeze through and got stuck, would they be crushed to death?

"What should we do?" Cindy asked anxiously.

"We have to get out," Sally said. "Go first, Cindy. You're the skinniest."

"You're as skinny as me," Cindy said.

"But I have big bones," Sally said.

"Shut up!" Adam snapped, dropping to his knees beside the shrinking hole. He tried pulling the closing edges apart with his hands. Contrary to what he had thought, the material had not turned molten. The rock was still hard as, well, rock. But it wasn't behaving like ordinary rock. It was like the tree that had tried to eat him his first day in Spooksville. It seemed to be alive. Adam pulled his hands back inside, afraid they would be crushed. He shouted out to Watch, who was peering in at them.

"Go find a stick!" Adam yelled. "Maybe we can prop it open!"

"Gotcha," Watch said and disappeared. He came back a few seconds later; by then the entrance was a foot wide. He had a short stubby stick and a couple of medium-size rocks. He tried using the stick as a brace, but the closing edges snapped it in two as if it were a twig. The girls screamed.

"Put in the rocks!" Adam cried desperately. "We can't let it seal us inside!"

"I don't know what's causing this!" Watch said, straining to fit the rocks in the shrinking gap. "Bill never said anything about the cave entrance closing."

"Bill is dead!" Sally yelled. "Just stop it from closing!"

Watch managed to get one rock in place. But the closing of the cave seemed unstoppable. For one second the stone balanced tensely between the sides of the opening. Then a crack appeared in the center of the rock, and suddenly it burst into dust. Adam had to wipe the debris from his eyes. He could hardly see as Watch shouted at him.

"I don't know how to stop it!" Watch said.

"Do you know why it started?" Adam shouted back.

Watch was barely visible. "No!"

"Go for help!" Adam cried just before his friend vanished.

"Where?"

"Go—" Adam began. But he was too late.

He was talking to a smooth black wall.

The cave entrance was closed.

They were trapped inside. In the dark.

4

THEY HAD TWO FLASHLIGHTS, SO IT WASN'T completely dark. The white beams reflected up over their grim features. But inside, where they really lived, all light had been extinguished. The cave had locked them in. And they had no reason to believe it would ever let them go. They sat in silence for several minutes by the vanished entrance, hardly peeking at one another. Finally Adam stirred. He was the boy, he told himself. He was responsible for keeping them from despairing.

"There might be another way out," he said.

"There isn't," Sally mumbled, staring at the ground.

"You don't know that for sure," Adam said. "We have to look."

"I don't want to look," Sally said. She gestured over her shoulder. "We might get eaten."

"Well, we can't sit here and do nothing." Adam was also staring at the ground. "Maybe we can dig our way out."

Sally felt the hard floor. "We'd need dynamite. Did you bring any?"

Adam felt the solid rock as well. It would take heavy equipment to drill through it. "No," he said quietly. "I forgot to bring any."

"I don't understand how this could have happened," Cindy whispered, her face pale.

"This is Spooksville," Sally said. "There's no understanding anything that happens here. The best you can do is not look for trouble." She added in a louder voice, "Like some of us wanted to do."

"You were the one who—" Cindy began.

"Let's not fight," Adam interrupted. "We don't have time." He tapped the side of his flashlight. "There isn't much energy in our batteries. If we don't find a way out before the lights give out, we'll never get out of here."

Sally sat up and stared hard at both of them. "I would like to hold one of the flashlights please."

"You can't have mine," Cindy said quickly.

"We'll stay together," Adam said. "It doesn't matter who carries the lights."

"Fine," Sally said. "Give me your light then."

"No," Adam said.

"Why not?" Sally asked. "I can hold it as well as you can. Give it to me."

"Why do you want it?" Cindy snapped.

"Because I'm afraid of the dark, bright brain," Sally said. Every kid who grew up in this town is. What do you need a light for? To fix your makeup?"

Adam held out his light. "Here. Take mine then, but turn it off. We'll use one light at a time to save batteries."

"I'll turn my light off first," Cindy said, catching Sally's eye. She nodded at her nemesis. "Because you're scared."

Sally nodded. "You'd better be scared, too."

Far below them, but maybe not so far away, they heard a faint noise again. Only this time it definitely sounded like a growl. The preying noise of some huge hungry creature. It echoed in their ears for ages before fading into a silence thicker than the blood that seemed to have turned to molasses in their hearts. Finally Adam swallowed and nodded in the direction of the sound.

"We have to go down that way," he said. "It's the only way out."

They started down, on their hands and knees this time. They were terrified of slipping. If they did, they might drop the flashlights. The bulbs might break, and then they wouldn't know what was in front of them, or what was coming at them from behind.

They reached the spot where they had turned back before, and it took a lot of courage to cross that line. Once over it they truly knew they couldn't go back. They moved as a single unit, practically holding on to each other.

"I wonder what Watch is doing," Cindy mumbled.

"He's walking home," Sally said. "Trying to figure out what to tell our parents."

"He could be going for help," Cindy said. "We could be rescued. Adam, maybe we should stay near the entrance."

Sally shook her head. "The authorities don't look for or rescue people in Spooksville. There are too many disappearances. They consider it a waste of time. Plus we lost half our police force in the last year."

"What happened to them?" Cindy asked.

Sally shrugged. "No one knows."

"Watch might be going to someone else for help," Adam said.

"Who would he ask?" Sally demanded, squeezing her light tight.

"Bum for one," Adam said. Then he added, "He might even go see Ann Templeton."

Sally sneered. "I'd rather face the creature down here than hope that evil witch would rescue us."

The creature might have heard Sally because it growled again. It definitely sounded hungry, maybe even excited. Perhaps it was coming their way, hoping to greet and eat them. The three of them stared at one another and Sally barely shook her head. She was taking back what she had just said, but it might have been too late for that.

5

ADAM KNEW HIS FRIEND WATCH WELL. WATCH did indeed go for help, and Bum was at the top of his list. Watch had a pretty good idea where Bum would be. It was Friday evening, and everyone knew it was Bum's custom to go to the only theater in town and try to sneak in to catch one of the new releases. But since the owner of the theater knew of Bum's habit, too, Bum was rarely successful at getting inside. Watch caught up with Bum just as he was being thrown out on the sidewalk.

"What's playing tonight?" Watch asked, helping his old friend up. Bum was dressed in his usual dirty gray coat and smelled as if he hadn't taken a bath in two weeks. But his bright green eyes had lost none of their humor. He laughed as he got to his feet.

"A horror film, as usual," Bum said. "It's a remake of *It: The Terror from Beyond*. The original was awful, so I don't mind missing the sequel." He paused and squinted at him. "How are you, Watch? You look worried."

Watch nodded. "I am. I took my friends up to the Haunted Cave and the entrance closed up on them. They're trapped inside."

Bum was amazed. "Why did you take them there?"

"Cindy Makey, the new girl in town, wanted to go."

"The one with the ghost for a granny?"

"Yeah, her. We saved her brother, but I don't know how we're going to save her now. Adam and Sally are with Cindy." Watch paused. It was never good to pressure Bum because he could clam up and tell you nothing. But Watch felt in a big hurry, which was unusual for him. "Do you know how to get the entrance to open up again?"

"Sure. You wait. It opens up again, eventually."

"How long does it take?"

Bum scratched his thinning hair. "Years."

"But they'll be dead by then."

"That is a problem." Bum leaned closer and spoke quietly. "Did you warn them about the Hyeets?"

"What's that?"

"The Bigfoots that live in the cave. They're a nasty lot. You know what happened to Bill Balley. The blasted creatures ate him alive. Ruined his final photo shoot."

Watch was concerned. "I didn't know they were called Hyeets, but I did warn the others about them."

Bum shrugged and looked down the block in the direction of the diner. "It doesn't matter if you warned them or not. The Hyeets will get them. Your friends are as good as dead. No sense worrying about them. Hey, how would you like to buy me dinner?"

Watch thought for a moment. "If I do, will you tell me everything you know about the Haunted Cave? And the Hyeets?"

"Deal." Bum grinned and slapped Watch on the back. "And if you get me dessert, I just might remember another way to get into the cave. You have money on you?"

Watch nodded and checked his watch set on West Coast time. The walk back to find Bum had been long and hard in the dark so his friends had been trapped for over an hour now. He wondered if he had put fresh batteries in the flashlights. Maybe he'd used old ones. He just hoped Bum could help in some way. At the moment Watch couldn't think of any other leads to pursue.

"I have money," Watch said almost to himself as they walked in the direction of the diner.

6

THE FLOOR HAD LEVELED OUT. THEY NO longer had to move forward on their hands and knees. The tunnel had also widened out so they weren't bumping into one another. These things were positive. Unfortunately the temperature had increased another ten degrees. They were sweating heavily and feeling terribly thirsty. Also, the flashlight Sally was carrying was beginning to dim. She shook it as they walked, trying to brighten the beam. They had been in the cave for two hours.

"This thing isn't going to last," Sally said.

Adam, walking on Sally's right, nodded. Cindy was on her left. "Let's just hope the second one has stronger batteries," he answered.

"It doesn't matter if it does if we don't know where we're going," Cindy said.

"You're a cheery character," Sally muttered.

"The queen of despair speaks," Cindy shot back.

"I would be at home watching TV and stuffing my face if you hadn't been so adamant about seeing this cave," Sally said.

"Just think of all the extra calories you're burning," Cindy replied.

"Would you two stop!" Adam said.

"Why should we stop?" Sally asked. "We're not low on oxygen. We might as well yell at each other in a desperate attempt to ward off the creeping horror that threatens to engulf our very souls."

"Well, if it makes you feel better," Adam said. But then his eyes took in a disturbing image. He stopped and pointed fifty feet up ahead. "What's that sticking out of the wall?" he asked, knowing the answer.

That was the arm of a skeleton. They approached it cautiously, with the light bobbing from Sally's trembling hand all the while. It was the last thing any of them wanted to find. The idea of being trapped inside the cave and eventually turning into skeletons was never far from their thoughts.

Yet this corpse didn't appear to have been trapped in

the cave, like them. "How could he have gotten in the wall?" Adam asked. Sally, of course, had her own theories.

"One of the ape creatures got him," she said. "Chewed him down to the bone, and stuffed him in there. It's obvious. It's probably what's going to happen to us."

"I don't know," Adam said. He nodded to Sally. "Give me the light."

"No," Sally said.

"I just want to look up ahead," Adam said.

"No," Sally said, hugging the flashlight close to her body.

"You can borrow Cindy's light until I come back," Adam said.

"She can't have mine," Cindy said quickly.

Adam frowned. "Then may I borrow your light?"

"Of course." Cindy handed it over. "What are you searching for?"

"Give me a minute and you'll see," Adam replied, flipping on the light. The glare from the second flashlight reminded them just how dim the first one was. Sally wanted to switch, but Adam wasn't in a negotiating mood. After telling the others to wait where they were, he moved carefully forward. Sally called after him.

"If something grabs you," she said, "scream real loud so we'll know to run the other way."

"Thanks," he muttered.

Two minutes and two hundred feet later, Adam found what he was looking for. It was a second skeleton, hanging partway out of the wall. Only this skeleton had portions of a rotting wooden box around him. Adam hurried back and collected the others, and then he showed them what he'd found. The girls were puzzled, and not too happy to see what they thought was a second victim of the ape creatures. But Adam shook his head.

"Don't you see?" he said. "This guy—if it was a guy— was buried in a coffin. The other corpse probably was as well, but his box just wore out over time."

Sally understood. "You're saying we're under the cemetery?"

"Exactly," Adam said.

"You act like that's good news," Sally said. "I mean, I can think of a lot better places to be."

"It's good that we know where we are," Adam explained.

"Why?" Sally asked.

"Maybe now we can plan which way to go," Adam said.

Sally gestured straight ahead of them. "It's only going one way, Adam. Straight to the monsters' kitchen."

"We'll see." Adam flicked off his flashlight. He was

shocked at how dark it was with only the first one on. They could hardly see one another. Yet the gloom gave him an idea. He reached out and yanked a board from the coffin out of the wall. The skeleton's skull bobbed up and down but the corpse didn't complain.

"What are you doing?" Sally asked. "That's the only home that guy's got, you know."

Adam continued to tug on the boards. "I want to take as many of these with us as we can. We have to prepare for both our lights running out. We might be able to use the wood as torches."

"That's a great idea," Cindy said, moving to help Adam.

"How are we going to light these torches?" Sally asked. "You're no Boy Scout, and Cindy and I are certainly not Girl Scouts. I couldn't kindle a spark into a campfire if you gave me a gallon of gasoline."

"Let's worry about that when we need to," Adam said.

Sally sighed, although she did begin to pull boards from the coffin. "This is great," she said. "When the ape creature goes to eat us, we can offer to build him a small house if he'll spare our lives."

Soon each of them had a small bundle of wood to carry. They started forward once more. They hadn't heard the creature growling in a while, and didn't know if that was a good sign or a bad one. In a way, Adam preferred it when the monster was making noise. At least then they knew where it was. There could be nothing worse than its sneaking up on them.

Five minutes after leaving the second skeleton, they came to a fork in the tunnel. They could go left or right. It was a difficult decision to make because both ways were dark and dangerous. Adam tried sniffing the air in each cave, searching for changes in temperature as well as foul odors. The cave on the right seemed to be cooler, but the one on the left was fresher smelling. He told the others what he had found. Of course the two girls immediately disagreed on which way to go.

"I want to go to the right," Cindy said. "We don't want to run into a lava pit."

"I think we should go to the left," Sally said. "The bad smell may be from things the ape creatures didn't completely eat."

"The right way doesn't actually smell bad," Cindy said, sniffing. "Its air is just stale."

"Dead things smell stale," Sally said.

"If we have just left the cemetery behind," Adam said, trying to get his directions straight, "then if we go right we should be right under the witch's castle."

"Then that settles it." Sally gasped. "We don't want to go anywhere near that place."

"But the castle has been there for ages," Adam said. "It might have a secret passage that leads down to this cave. We could use it to get out."

"And end up where?" Sally complained. "In the witch's living room. She'll roast us in her fireplace."

"You're thinking of the witch who looked like her on the other side of the Secret Path," Adam said. "Ann Templeton doesn't seem all that bad."

Sally shook her head. "I can't believe you. Ann Templeton smiled at you and told you you had beautiful eyes and you want to disregard all the evil things she's done to the kids in this town."

"I think you've made up half those things," Adam said.

"Maybe I have," Sally said. "But if the other half is true, you still don't want to get near her."

"I want to try my luck with the castle," Cindy said firmly. "I'm tired and thirsty. I don't know how much longer I can keep going like this."

"I'm not going that way," Sally said just as firmly.

"You have to," Adam said. "Your light is about to run out."

Sally sounded hurt. "You would leave me here alone in the dark to die? Just because Cindy wants to go right and

I want to go left? Adam, I thought you were my friend."

"I'm not leaving you to die," Adam said patiently. "We have to go one way or the other. If this way doesn't work out, we can come back and try your way."

Sally sighed again. "I have a bad feeling about this."

"You have bad feelings twenty-four hours a day," Cindy muttered.

"If you had grown up in this town you would understand," Sally replied.

7

THE SPACE NARROWED AS THEY TURNED TO
the right, and the temperature definitely fell. In fact,
it began to feel very cool. Adam took that as a good
sign. He stopped feeling so thirsty. But the clock was
still ticking. They couldn't wander around forever. Their
first flashlight was all but dead. To keep from bumping
into one another, they had to turn on the second. Adam
told Sally to save what little was left of the batteries in
the first. She turned it off and put it in her back pocket.

Ten minutes after leaving the fork, they came to a
huge open area. For a second Adam was ready to celebrate. He thought they had gotten out of the cave alto-
gether. But after setting down his sticks and searching

around with the beam of Cindy's light, he realized they weren't home yet. It was as if a large mine shaft had been sunk into the ground, and they had stumbled into the bottom of it. Circular walls surrounded them. But his light was not strong enough to reveal what was at the top of the shaft and how high up it went.

Adam saw that the cave did not continue on the other side.

There was only one way in, one way out.

"Where are we?" Cindy whispered.

"We may be under the castle," Adam said. "Do you think I should call out?"

"No," Sally said.

"Yes," Cindy said.

"Do what Cindy says," Sally whined. "You always do."

"That's not fair," Cindy snapped. "Adam's his own person. He makes his own decisions."

"Shh." Adam held up his hand. "I think I hear something."

What he heard was the faint clanging of metal. It seemed to be coming from directly overhead and on opposite sides of the shaft—two sources. Adam was reminded of the black knight on the other side of the Secret Path, the servant of the evil redheaded witch. The knight had creaked like an unoiled hinge as he walked. The people—or creatures—above them now did as well.

Faint orange lights began to glow a hundred feet above them on both sides of the shaft. Clearly there were two people approaching the shaft from opposite tunnels. But the sound of their heavy armor—for that was what it sounded like to him—worried Adam. He was on the verge of telling the girls to back out of the shaft when the flames of two torches seemingly burst out from the walls of the shaft. In reality, there was a narrow stone walkway far above them that the two creatures had stepped onto.

And they were definitely creatures, not humans.

They were man-size trolls. Their faces were squished and ugly. They looked as if their mothers had been lizards married to pigs. They had fat flat noses and angry red eyes that smoked with anger. They wore smooth steel breastplates, and in their right hands they carried broad silver swords. With their left hands, they held up their flaming torches. They gloated when they saw what had stumbled into their pit.

That was how Adam felt. As if they had stumbled into a trap.

He shouted at the girls. "Run back to the cave!"

They dashed for the opening, but before they could reach it a gate of metal bars fell down over the opening.

It smashed into the dirt floor, piercing the ground with long spikes. They all three tugged on it as hard as they could, but it refused to budge. Overhead Adam saw one of the trolls set his sword and torch down and reach for a long black spear. There was a chain attached to the base. Even before the troll attacked, it was clear what he and his partner intended to do. To spear the foolish human kids and haul them up to have for dinner. The creatures wanted their meat. Alive or dead.

The troll raised the spear over his head.

"Duck!" Adam cried to the girls.

The three of them hit the floor.

The spear struck the metal gate with a loud clang.

Sparks flew. They all cried out.

The troll had missed. But he didn't mind.

He would have all the chances he needed to catch them.

The troll pulled the spear back up by yanking on the chain attached to the base of it.

Adam leaped up. "Spread out," he called. "Keep moving. Make yourself a difficult target."

The shaft was maybe a hundred feet across. That was wide, but with two trolls standing above, Adam felt as if they were trapped in a narrow crevasse. The overhead walkway clearly circled the entire shaft. The troll with the torch helped his partner. While the one with the spear aimed, the other held the light out for him to get a clear view of his victim. Adam saw that they were aiming for him.

The troll threw his spear once more.

Adam jumped to the right.

The spear went through the space between his left arm and his left side. It tore his shirt; it had missed him by inches. The trolls laughed and their slobber dripped down into the shaft. They were enjoying the sport. Adam was so scared he couldn't move. Not even as the troll pulled the spear back up to where he was standing. The two trolls shifted position. They were going after Cindy next.

"Keep moving!" Adam shouted again, remembering to find his own feet.

But Cindy did the worst of all things. Staring up at the troll with the spear, terror in her eyes, she backed up against the stone wall. Standing almost still, she made a perfect target. Overhead, the troll raised his spear once more. Adam knew what was about to happen, but was too far away to stop it.

"Cindy!" he screamed. "Duck!"

She didn't. The spear flew through the dark air, headed right for her heart. Adam wanted to close his eyes. He couldn't bear to see her die.

But then, suddenly, Cindy went flying off to one side. Sally had tackled her.

The spear hit the rock wall and fell harmlessly to the ground.

Adam pumped his fist. "Yeah! Way to go Sally!"

Sally and Cindy jumped back up in an instant.

"You save me next time," Sally muttered, keeping her eyes on the trolls.

"Deal," Cindy said, gasping.

Adam ran over to them. "I have an idea," he said quietly. "But to make it work we have to gather back by the metal gate."

"They'll get one of us for sure if we do that," Sally protested.

"They'll get us all if we don't do something drastic," Adam said. "Trust me on this."

They hurried to the entrance. Already the troll had his spear back in hand. He laughed when he saw them standing so close together, standing so still. He drew back his arm.

"Jump to the side just as he lets go," Adam whispered, standing between the two girls.

"Which way are you jumping?" Sally asked on his right.

"You'll see," Adam said, reaching behind him and grabbing two bars of the metal gate.

The troll let his spear go.

It flew toward Adam.

Adam had known the troll would aim for him, since he was in the middle. He also thought the troll would aim low, figuring the stupid human boy would try ducking again. For that reason, Adam pulled himself up on the bars just as the spear flew toward him. He almost didn't pull himself up in time. The blade on the spear scratched his left leg as it stabbed past, drawing blood beside his knee. But Adam didn't mind because the spear landed exactly where he wanted it to. On the other side of the gate. As the troll growled and started to pull the spear back up, Adam jumped down and grabbed the spear.

Now Adam knew he was no match—strength-wise—for a troll. If he had a tug-of-war with the creature for the spear, he'd lose. Adam had something more clever up his sleeve. Before the troll could react, Adam pulled the tip of the spear out of the dirt, passed it and the chain it was attached to around one of the metal bars, and jammed it back into the ground.

Overhead the troll yanked hard.

But the spear stayed where Adam had jammed it.

The girls jumped to Adam's side and patted him on the back.

"Absolutely brilliant," Sally said.

"You're hero material," Cindy agreed.

"Let's not celebrate yet," Adam said quietly. "We can't push this gate up by ourselves, but maybe we can get the trolls to lift it for us. We have to get them real mad so they're not thinking. I just want them anxious to get their spear back."

"How do you get a troll mad?" Cindy asked.

"Just watch me," Sally said, turning to face their tormentors. She spoke in a loud, mocking voice. For once Adam was glad to hear it. "Oh, Mr. Trolls! It doesn't look like you'll be having dinner tonight. That's too bad. I feel real sorry for you guys. I know it must be a drag having to work down here in this dark dungeon. You're always on the night shift. I bet you guys never get out and see the sun. I can tell that just by looking at you. I mean, really, you guys are ugly. You're disgustingly gross. You look like frogs that swallowed too many hormones. Lizards that sucked up too much slime. I bet you guys can't even get a date with a girl troll. That hair sticking out of your noses is disgusting. You both need to see a barber. And didn't your mothers teach you any manners when you were baby trolls? You're not supposed to slobber over your food until you've killed it and drawn it out of the pit. It's lousy etiquette, plain and simple. A goblin would never behave that way."

Sally's antics had the desired effect. Even though they didn't understand exactly what she said, the trolls were instantly furious. They growled bitterly and their slobber dripped all over the place. They circled the overhead walkway until they were standing directly above the metal gate. Of course that was exactly what Adam was hoping for. Because as the trolls yanked hard on the chain, the chain slowly began to lift the gate upward. A crack appeared beneath the barrier, then a foot of space—two feet. That was enough for Adam.

"Get under it!" he shouted. Letting the girls go first, Adam grabbed several of the boards from the coffin and slid under the gate just behind Cindy. Above him he could hear the trolls screaming in anger. They released their hold on the chain, and the gate clanged down once more. But by then Adam and his friends were free, racing away at high speed and gasping with relief.

"I told you we should go to the left," Sally said, panting.

"You can say I told you so as many times as you want," Cindy said.

"As long as the other way doesn't turn out to be worse," Adam agreed.

8

WATCH HAD FED BUM A TURKEY DINNER complete with mashed potatoes, gravy, and stuffing and still he hadn't learned anything that could help free his friends from the Haunted Cave. Bum was simply too interested in his food to be worried about such trivial matters as three trapped kids. The way Bum shoveled down his white meat and buttered biscuits, Watch suspected he hadn't eaten a decent meal in a week.

"Would you like anything else?" Watch asked, growing impatient. He hadn't ordered food for himself, only a glass of milk, which tasted flat and chalky, like something out of Mr. Spiney's refrigerator. Mr. Spiney, the town librarian, always added calcium to the milk he made everyone drink so that it would make one's bones stronger. Mr. Spiney had a thing about strong bones, although he had lousy posture himself.

Bum nodded with a mouthful of food. "I'll have apple pie and ice cream as soon as I finish with this." He paused to look at Watch. "Are you sure you're not hungry?"

Watch lowered his head. "I'm not feeling hungry at all."

Bum nodded. "You're worried about your friends, I understand. Maybe I was a little hasty when I said to forget about trying to rescue them." He picked up his glass of water. Even though he was Spooksville's town bum, he never actually drank alcohol. He took a sip of his water and continued. "Maybe there's another way into the cave."

"You mentioned that earlier," Watch said, sitting up straight. "Do you know another way?"

Bum burped and picked at his potatoes. "No."

Watch fell back in his seat. "Oh."

"But because I don't know of one doesn't mean it doesn't exist." Bum paused. "Ann Templeton might know another way in."

"The town witch?"

"Yeah. She's a clever gal."

Watch removed his thick glasses and cleaned them on

his shirt. They often steamed up. "Did she really put a curse on you so you went from being town mayor to town bum?"

Bum chuckled. "If she did curse me, I was happy for it. Being a bum is much more fun than being mayor. You never have to attend any meetings. I used to hate all those meetings. People would sit around a table and talk about things none of them had the slightest interest in. It made me want to set city hall on fire."

"I thought you did set city hall on fire."

Bum scratched his chin. "Oh, yeah, that's right. That was the night the fire chief's wife was having her baby. City hall was always so ugly. I think the ash did more for it than a fresh coat of paint would have."

Watch put his glasses back on. Without them, he was legally blind. He hadn't been able to see well since his family had broken up and spread to all parts of the country. But that wasn't something he talked about with others. Even Sally did not know what he had gone through growing up in Spooksville. Watch had not had an easy childhood.

"Did you ever annoy Ann Templeton?" Watch asked. "If we're going to ask her for a favor, I'd like to know ahead of time."

Bum ran his hand through his stringy hair. "Well, I once proposed to the city council that we pave over the local cemetery and build a rec center on top of it. Since the cemetery is practically in her backyard, that might have made her mad. She did send me a skull in the mail the day after I made the proposal. I used it as a paperweight for a month or two, until I was replaced,"

"Why did you want to put a rec center on top of a cemetery?" Watch asked.

Bum burst out laughing and slapped his knee. "I thought we could have wonderful Halloween parties with all those dead people beneath us!"

Watch had to smile. "The place does have a nice view. But back to talking to Ann Templeton. Do you know where she is right now?"

Bum glanced at one of Watch's watches. The service at the diner was awful. It had taken forever to get Bum's food. Over three hours had passed since Watch last saw his friends. It was close to eleven.

"At twelve she'll go to the grocery store," Bum said. "She always buys her food on Friday at midnight. She doesn't trust any of her servants to do the shopping. She doesn't have many human ones anyway. The store stays open just for her in fact. They're afraid to close until she's done with her business. Once they did shut early on a Friday, and the next day the meat cutter was found frozen to death in the meat locker."

"Did he have a meat hook through his brain?" Watch asked.

"No. He had choked to death on an ice-cream bar. Whether it was her fault, I don't know. But they always treat her real nice at the market."

"Earlier you called the ape creatures in the cave Hyeets," Watch said. "Where does that name come from?"

"That's what the Native Americans who used to live around here called the creatures," Bum explained. "They really are the Bigfoots the TV programs sometimes do special reports on. They're the missing link—the bridge between humans and apes. You have to respect them. They get more press than most of our local politicians."

"Are they intelligent?" Watch asked.

Bum was thoughtful. "I don't know. They're always hungry, that's for sure. But since they live underground where there's not much food, they can't be too smart."

Watch hesitated. "Do they really eat people?"

Bum nodded seriously and returned to his food. "Yeah, they like kids the best. Those they can't get enough of."

9

ADAM AND HIS FRIENDS WERE TWO HOURS on the left-hand tunnel before they came to another fork. This time there were three choices. The cave on the right curved down. The middle tunnel continued on a level plane, and the one on the left curved up. They all had different opinions about which way to go.

"I want to go to the left," Cindy said. "The more we go up the more chance we have of reaching the surface."

Sally stepped into Cindy's tunnel. She sniffed the air and frowned. "It stinks in here."

Adam had to agree. "It does smell like there's a dead animal down that way. I think we should go to the right. I know it slants down, but there is fresh air blowing out of it. It could open to the outside."

"No way," Sally said. "We can't go down and we can't go in the direction of dead animals. I say we take the middle route, and you should do what I say because look what happened last time when we listened to Cindy."

"Last time I wanted to go to the right as well," Adam reminded her.

"Only because she whispered the word in your ear," Sally said.

"I would resent that except you just saved my life," Cindy replied.

"And don't you forget it, sister," Sally said.

Adam was undecided. They had been using their second flashlight a long time. The batteries seemed to be holding out pretty well, but they wouldn't last forever. They were all very tired, very thirsty. Each time they paused to rest, they took longer to get up. Adam worried that soon they wouldn't be able to get up at all.

It wasn't just the cool air that made him want to take the downward path. Far away, ever so faintly, he thought he heard the rushing of water. He believed if there was an underground stream, it might eventually lead to the outside. All they would have to do was follow it. Plus they could take care of their thirst. Unfortunately, when he asked the others to listen for the sound of water, they couldn't hear a thing.

"I think you're just so thirsty you're hallucinating," Sally said.

Adam was afraid she might be right, for once. "Are you sure you don't hear it, Cindy?" he asked.

"I'm sorry, Adam," Cindy said. "I don't hear a thing. Plus I just can't see going down. Let's go to the left."

"To the center," Sally insisted.

They were waiting for him to make the final decision. At the moment Adam wished they had another leader. If he made the wrong choice, the chances were he would kill them all. Going against his gut feeling, he nodded toward the middle cave.

"We'll continue this way," he said. "See what happens."

At first there was no change in scenery. The cave continued straight and level. Another hour of thirsty walking went by. They began to lean on one another for support. Adam was still carrying several of the boards from the coffin, and they kept getting heavier and heavier. He was tempted to put them down, but Cindy's flashlight had begun to dim slightly. He tried not to think what it would be like to be trapped, wandering around in the dark. Why, they could come to the edge of a cliff and just walk off it, without realizing it until they were falling.

The middle cave was not without its bad smells, either.

The odor hit them before they saw it.

They found their first dead bat.

They hadn't seen any living ones, of course, but this dead one filled them with dark fear. Adam borrowed the light from Cindy to examine it closer. Other bats had not killed this bat. It was clear that a large creature had torn it open in one swift jerk. There was blood all around it, and the blood, although not fresh, was not dry either.

The bat had sharp tiny teeth.

He wondered if it was a bloodsucker.

"How long ago did it die?" Sally asked, for once standing close to Cindy. Adam sat back from the disgusting remains and frowned.

"Maybe a day," he said.

"It doesn't look like it committed suicide," Sally said.

"No," Adam said, climbing to his feet and handing the flashlight back to Cindy. "I think one of the ape creatures got it." He paused. "Do you still want to go this way, Sally?"

She seemed to be exhausted. Her dark hair clung to the sides of her face like streaks of dirt. Her lips were dry and cracked. Adam's own knee was bleeding slightly from the brush with the troll's spear. But he hadn't told the girls about the wound. It was the last of his worries. Sally shook her head.

"I don't have the energy left to walk back the way we came," she said.

"Do you have the energy to fight what killed the bat?" Cindy asked. She added softly, "We should have gone to the left."

"We shouldn't have come into the cave at all," Sally snapped. "This wasn't my brilliant idea." Yet she didn't have the strength to continue arguing. She hung her head wearily, looking at the bat once more. "You decide, Adam. I can't."

He shook his head. "We've already decided. We can only go forward."

Forward quickly got more gruesome. Spider webs appeared. Not the annoying little things they saw around their yards or garages from time to time. These were massive webs. They spanned the width of the cave. To keep going, Adam had to remove his shirt to swipe at them. And sometimes the spiders would come running out and snap at them with tiny black claws and greasy red eyes. They saw one spider that was as large as a small rabbit. But it ran away when Adam threw a rock at it.

The temperature increased. Thirst and exhaustion were all they knew. Adam tried to figure out what time it was but was unable to focus long enough. It felt as if they had been trapped in the cave for weeks. Briefly he wondered if

Watch had talked to his parents, if his mom and dad were planning his funeral. At least they wouldn't have to pay for a coffin, he thought. The entire cave could be his tomb.

They stumbled upon another two dead bats. Adam knelt to examine them. They didn't smell as bad as the first one because their blood was fresher. They had been killed in exactly the same way as the first one. The girls waited anxiously for his opinion. He was afraid to give it.

"Well?" Sally said impatiently.

"I think these bats died in the last two hours," he said.

"Did they die here?" Cindy asked.

"Looks like it," Adam said, standing back up.

Cindy's voice cracked as she spoke. "That means one of those creatures was just here."

"What it really means is one of those creatures is not far from here," Sally said.

"But we haven't heard it in a while," Adam said.

Sally's eyes shifted from side to side. "I've been hearing something. Faint steps that pause when we pause. And I've felt eyes on me. You know what it's like when someone's staring at you behind your back. You can feel it. Well, something is staring at us."

"You're imagining it," Cindy said quickly.

Sally pointed at the dead bats. "Am I imagining that? I'm telling you the truth, I think we've been followed for a while."

"Why didn't you say something earlier?" Adam asked.

"What good would it do?" Sally asked.

Adam glanced up and down the tunnel, using the beam of the flashlight to pierce the darkness. Beyond the light's range there was only darkness and spiders and probably more dead bats.

"If it is following us," he said, "and it hasn't attacked yet, that might mean it doesn't want to attack."

"That's wishful thinking," Sally said. She also looked around and then shivered, although she seemed ready to fall over from heat exhaustion. "But I suppose that's the best kind of thinking we can have right now."

Cindy wrinkled her nose at the bloody bats. "One thing's for sure—the bat killer is not a vegetarian."

Sally nodded grimly. "It probably doesn't even like ice cream."

They continued on. The air was so dry now it was hard to swallow. Another odor floated through the air. It had probably always been there, but they had just gotten used to it. Now it was too strong to ignore. They were definitely approaching some kind of active volcanic area. Tiny black cinders floated in the air before them and caught in their hair. The odor and the cinders made it harder to breathe. They were all coughing.

Then the black cloud came.

They had seen dead bats, but no live ones, and that

had made Adam wonder. Soon he would wonder no more. They were taking a short rest when Adam heard a faint flapping above them. He was the first to hear it. As the sound grew louder, it took on a peculiar humming quality. For a moment he wondered if he was listening to a swarm of bees. The girls turned to him.

"What's that?" Sally asked nervously.

Adam jumped up and shone his flashlight in the direction of the sound. Actually, it was coming from behind them, from the length of the tunnel they had just walked. At first he couldn't see anything except the remains of the spider webs they had pushed through. But then all of a sudden the webs began to shake violently. One huge spider, hanging on to what was left of its broken home, turned to shreds in midair. Something *new* was pushing through the webs. Something with several thousand black wings and a million pairs of beady red eyes.

A swarm of bats was coming.

Coming right toward them.

"Run!" Adam shouted, pushing the girls in front of him.

They ran as fast as they could, but they were no match for winged creatures. The bats were on them in a minute and the horror of it was beyond imagining. They were in their hair, under their shirts, pecking at their ears and fingers. Adam felt the claws of a bat land on his closed eyes. He brushed it away but two took its place. He remembered the tiny sharp teeth of the dead bats and a second later he felt them as several bats tried to bite into his skin. He wanted to scream louder than he had ever screamed in his entire life, but he was afraid a bat would fly into his mouth.

The bats were thirsty. They wanted blood.

What a way to die. Such a horrible death.

Yet all was not lost. Adam accidentally opened one eye and caught a faint glimpse of a strange red light fifty feet ahead. It flashed out from a narrow crack in the wall of the cave. Curiously enough, there were no bats around this light. That was enough for Adam. He grabbed the girls' arms as they continued to wave them to keep from being eaten alive.

"I see a way out!" he shouted. "Come with me!"

He pulled the stumbling girls after him. The bats followed, of course, since they were thirsty little devils. Yet as they moved within ten feet of the smoldering orange crack in the wall, the bats veered away. Adam assumed they didn't like the smell, or else the wicked red light disturbed them. He squeezed through the crack first, pulling the girls in behind him.

They took a second to get their bearings.

They were standing in a huge volcanic chamber.

10

Spooksville's largest grocery store was called Fred's Foods. Fred himself was a bagger at the store—he had been for thirty years. He owned the place but couldn't figure out how to work the cash registers or do anything else useful. So he bagged groceries and helped people out to their cars. It was lucky for Fred that he had hired an assistant manager with half a brain, or else the place would have closed down ages ago.

Watch and Bum found Ms. Ann Templeton in the produce department, knocking lightly on watermelons. She wore an expensive white pantsuit, shiny black shoes, and exquisite diamond earrings. Her long black hair was curly; it reached almost to her waist. Her face, as she glanced over at them and smiled, was as beautiful as always, and as pale. She was either an angel from heaven, or a ghost from a much lower place. Her dark eyes shone with wicked amusement. She couldn't have been more than thirty years old.

"Watch and Bum," she said in her soft yet powerful voice. "Have you come to help carry my groceries to my car? I could use some help this fine evening. I think poor old Fred has already left for the day."

Bum bowed slightly. "I wouldn't mind helping you with your food, ma'am, if you could spare me a loaf of bread or two."

"I will give you a can of tuna," Ms. Templeton said. She studied him and frowned at his appearance. "I think you could use some fish. Your skin looks terrible."

"It's the sleeping outdoors every night that does it," Bum said.

"There are worse places to sleep, I suppose." She returned to knocking on watermelons. "Looking for your friends, Watch?"

Watch almost jumped out of his socks. "Yeah. How did you know they were missing?"

"Nothing happens in Spooksville that I don't know about. Isn't that true, Bum?"

"Yeah, ma'am. No one puts anything past you."

Ms. Templeton continued. "Your friends somehow managed to sneak into my basement, Watch. I should say it was one of my *lower* basements, not the best way to enter my castle, if you're a human being. I am sorry to say that they were not given the most hospitable welcome."

"What happened?" Watch asked, worried.

"A couple of my boys tried to have them for dinner." Ms. Templeton smiled. "It is so hard to find good help these days. I don't know what the world's coming to."

Watch gulped. "Are they dead?"

Ms. Templeton chuckled. "Heavens no. Thanks to Adam, they escaped. I'm sure they're still wandering around down there somewhere, unless the bats or Hyeets have eaten them."

Watch took a step forward. "Can you help me rescue them?" He added, "I'll help carry your groceries out to your car for the next two months."

Ms. Templeton threw her head back and laughed. "If I help you that will spoil all the fun. Watch, you wouldn't want that. It wouldn't be fair to them."

"But you said it yourself, they might die."

Ms. Templeton shrugged. "Lots of people die in this town. I can't be responsible for all of them." She picked up a plump watermelon. "Now this one looks ripe."

"But I thought you liked Adam," Watch protested.

"What made you think that?" Ms. Templeton asked.

"I don't know," Watch said. "He likes you."

She glanced over. "Really?"

Watch nodded. "Yeah. He thinks you're real pretty. It drives Sally crazy."

Ms. Templeton was amused. "It's fun to see Sally lose her temper. She reminds me of myself when I was young." She paused. "Do you know what I used to do when I was your age, Watch? Just for fun?"

Bum shook his head. "I remember."

"I'm sure you do," she said. "And I'm sure you're glad I never did it to you. In those days, Watch, I was fond of hiking in the caves with several of the kids at school. I would dare them to join me, usually boys who made fun of my family. Then when we were a mile or two underground, I would make all their flashlights fail. It would scare them so bad they would start crying and screaming for help. Just like little babies."

"Would you help them?" Watch asked.

Ms. Templeton set the watermelon in her cart. "Sometimes, but not often. I think a lot of those kids are still down there, in the bellies of the Hyeets." She laughed when she saw Watch's confused expression. "All right, since Adam thinks I'm so pretty, I will give you a couple of hints that might help you rescue them."

Watch looked around for pen and paper. "Do I need to take notes?"

"No, just listen," Ms. Templeton said. "The entrance to the cave closed up on Adam and his friends, right?"

"Right," Watch said. "For no reason."

She shook her head. "There was a reason. The Haunted Cave is sensitive. It does what you tell it. Someone must have accidentally told the cave to close."

"No," Watch disagreed. "No one said anything about—"

But then he stopped, remembering the words Cindy had shouted at Sally. Even though he had been standing outside the cave, he had heard them loud and clear.

Yeah, but you've got a poison tongue. I wish for just once you would shut up. That you would close your mouth, shut it tight . . .

Watch continued. "Cindy did say something about shutting tight. She was talking about Sally's mouth, but the cave did start to close right then."

"That's it," Ms. Templeton said. "The cave thought you wanted it to close up. So it did."

"Then all we have to do is return to the entrance and command it to open?" Watch asked.

"That works some of the time," she said thoughtfully. "But a tribe of Native Americans lived here long before Europeans came, and the cave is more receptive to their language. They were called the Reeksvars. They named the Hyeets and many other strange creatures in this area. Their word for open was *Bela*. Their word for close was *Nela*. It's always good to know how to close whatever you happen to open. If you shout *Bela* to the cave, it will open right away." She paused. "But your friends are nowhere near that entrance by the reservoir. They've been walking all night. If you go there, you won't find them."

Watch felt frustrated. "Is there another way into the cave?"

Ms. Templeton mocked him. "You can always try my lower basement. But I can't guarantee you'll make it past my boys. Adam and his friends got them all riled up. I'm going to have to buy them a dozen boxes of Ritz crackers just to calm them down."

"They like crackers?" Watch asked, confused about exactly who or what her *boys* were.

"Yes," she said. "Very much, with snails and spiders. But to return to your question, there are several entrances to the cave. You just have to know how to find them." She leaned over and spoke softly in his ear. "I will give you one more hint, Watch. The wells in this town run deep. The waters run cold. It is hot where your friends now walk, but soon they will be able to soothe their thirst. If they're lucky."

Watch brightened. "Then they are alive."

Ms. Templeton stood back up and nodded. "They're alive for now. But the night is far from over. The Hyeets hunt at night. If they run into one, there's no telling what will happen."

"But I don't understand your hint," Watch said. "I still don't know how to get to them."

She patted him on the head. "That's your problem." She handed Bum a can of tuna. "Good night, Bum. Good night, Watch. You can help me with my groceries next time. I will remember your promise. And you remember me, whenever you are eager for strange dreams or exciting adventures."

"Have a fine evening, ma'am," Bum said, holding on to the can of tuna as if it were a rose from a girlfriend. He grabbed Watch by the arm as Ms. Templeton disappeared around another aisle. "I heard what she said to you. You don't want to push her. Her moods are quick to change. She might put a curse on you. She told us more than I thought she would."

"Do you know how we can reach Adam and the others?" Watch asked.

Bum nodded. "Based on what she said, I have an idea."

11

THE CHAMBER WAS AS WIDE AND HIGH AS A high-school auditorium. There was not one but a half-dozen pools of glowing lava spread about the stone room. Steam rose from the glowing liquid rock, gathering near the ceiling of the chamber, forming a shimmering cloud of sparks and fumes. Every few seconds a miniature geyser would spurt up from one of the molten pools and splash the surrounding black rock. The place was as hot as an oven. They were able to see clearly without their flashlight, but the sober red glow had a strange effect on them. It was as if they had died and gone to an evil place. Sally said it for all of them when she spoke next.

"I hope there are no devils in here," she said.

"I don't believe in devils," Cindy said quickly.

"I would think you would believe in everything after tonight," Sally said, wiping at a bloody scratch on her face. "I'm just happy we got away from those bats. I think they were vampires."

"Spooksville would have no other kind," Adam agreed, also wiping at his face and arms. He had a dozen small scratches, but none were serious. The bats had been the hardest on Cindy. She had several big bites in her left ear. Adam had to admire her. The bites were bleeding but she wasn't complaining.

Although the light from the lava pits was reassuring, the fumes in the place made it hard to breathe. They were pretty much constantly coughing, and their thirst was a real problem now. After the bat attack, they felt even more dehydrated. Adam noticed the girls beginning to wobble on their feet. He was having trouble focusing his own eyes. Plus he was beginning to get a headache. He nodded at the chamber.

"Let's explore this place quickly," he said. "But if we don't find anything that can help us, then we have to go back into the cave."

"But the bats are in the cave," Sally protested.

"We have no choice," Adam said. "Besides they might have flown off. We might not see them again."

"If they catch us away from here," Cindy said, "we're dead."

"You took the words right out of my mouth," Sally said.

They had been exploring the chamber only a couple of minutes when they found a strange set of four lines on the far wall. They made the shape of a large doorlike rectangle, and were etched into the rock. The bottom line started two feet above the floor and ran parallel to it. The top had to be twelve feet above them. It was a big door, perhaps for huge creatures to go in and out. But it wasn't really a door, just lines on a wall. Like a caveman's drawing. They exchanged puzzled glances.

"Somebody cut these into the rock," Adam said.

"What for?" Sally asked.

"Your guess is as good as mine," Adam said.

Sally reached out and touched the sharp-edged grooves. They were about two inches deep, straight, and without flaws. The surrounding volcanic stone was hard. It would have taken a powerful instrument to cut the lines.

"The person who drew these was not just doodling," Sally said. "This could be a door of some kind. A portal to another place."

"But it has no hinges," Cindy said. "No doorknob."

"Interdimensional portals don't need hinges or door-knobs," Sally said. "Adam and I have had experience with this kind of thing before. When we passed through the Secret Path."

Adam nodded. "But that portal took us into a night-mare world. I wonder if this doorway would do the same—if we knew how to open it."

Cindy spoke with feeling. "We already are in a night-mare world. If we can open it, then we should open it." She coughed, choked actually. Her voice came out weak and dry. "I need water real bad."

"I wouldn't mind a tall glass of ginger ale myself," Sally said. She glanced at Adam. "Can you think of any special spells to open this door?"

Adam shook his head. "With the Secret Path, we just had to walk backward into the tombstone to make it work."

"Not really," Sally said. "First we had to trek all over town in a certain order." She paused. "But if you want to try walking backward into the thing, I'm all for it."

Together, the three of them tried the technique that had worked so well in the graveyard. But they just ended up bumping their heads on the hard stone wall. Adam was not enthusiastic about experimenting any more.

"We're dripping sweat even when we stand still," he

said. "We're going to lose what water our bodies have left if we don't get out of here."

"But that tunnel in the cave was leading us nowhere," Sally protested. "We have to give this a chance."

"What should we do?" Adam asked simply.

Sally threw up her arms. "I don't know. Let me fool with it for a bit. You guys go sit closer to the cave, where it's cooler. Please, Adam, give me at least ten minutes."

"No more," Adam warned. "You'll pass out if you stay any longer." He surveyed the bubbling pools as he wiped the sweat from his face. "I wonder if the ape creatures ever come here?"

It was an interesting question to ask.

Perhaps it was the wrong question.

Adam rested with Cindy by the crack in the cave wall that led into the volcanic chamber. They sat outside, on the cave side. There the temperature was still warm, but at least it wasn't blasting like a furnace. They stared at each other, probably wondering which one of them looked worse. Cindy's blond hair was covered with black soot. The blood from her ear had spilled onto her white blouse. Her lips were cracked and starting to bleed. Her eyes were so weary, she looked as if she hadn't slept in days.

"Are we going to get out of here?" she asked after a minute of silence.

Adam sighed. "I don't know. There could be an exit just around the next curve, or the cave tunnels could go on for another ten miles. But we've been walking under Spooksville for the last few hours, and I can't imagine that the caves run under the ocean. For that reason, I think we're going to reach the end of the road, one way or the other."

"You mean the cave might just end in a wall?" Cindy asked.

"Or it might end in someone's backyard. It's possible."

Cindy was doubtful. "But we don't know of anyone who has a cave opening in their backyard."

Adam nodded reluctantly. "That's true. If the cave does have an exit inside the city, then it's where no one knows about it."

Cindy shook her head sadly, fingering the flashlight. They didn't need it turned on here. But the moment they left this area it would be their only source of illumination. Adam thought the batteries couldn't last more than another hour.

"This is all my fault," she said quietly. "I forced us into this cave."

"You didn't force me. I wanted to come."

Cindy smiled faintly. "That's nice of you to say,

Adam, but I think I forced you more than anyone. I just assumed you'd come. And you did." She paused. "Why?"

He shrugged. "It sounded like an interesting adventure."

"But you've had plenty of those since you moved here." She paused again. "Did you come because you thought I'd think you were a coward if you didn't?"

"No," he said. Then he added, "Maybe."

Cindy laughed softly. "I could never think that. You're the bravest boy I've ever met."

"Really?" That was nice to hear.

Cindy touched his knee. "Of course. Who else our age would swim with sharks and fight with ghosts and wrestle with trolls?"

"Sally."

Cindy giggled. "Sally's weird. I don't really hate her, you know. I just love to tease her. She has so many buttons, and I can't stop pushing them."

"I think she cares about you, too. You saw the way she risked her life to save you from that troll's spear?"

Cindy nodded. "I just hope I don't need to be saved again."

It may have been the wrong thing to say.

Especially considering where they were sitting.

Adam didn't know exactly what happened next.

The cave around them was black, of course. Everything underground was black. But it seemed as if for a moment a deeper blackness rose up from some hidden depths. The shadow came from one side, and it swiftly took on a vague shape. Adam saw a hairy face, yellow teeth, weird eyes—yet it was all a blur. Before he could react, even shout, the shadow fell on Cindy. It covered her in darkness and then quickly pulled back into the black. Cindy wasn't given a chance to scream. Adam wasn't given a chance to save her.

She was just gone.

The monster had her.

12

BUM KNEW ABOUT A WELL LOCATED NOT far from the beach. He believed it was one of the wells Ann Templeton had been referring to. Watch had never heard of the place, and he knew the town inside and out. Or at least he thought he did. But Bum explained why he had never seen it before.

"It's located in an old woman's backyard," Bum said. "Her name's Mrs. Robinson. She never leaves her house. When her husband died ten years ago, she didn't even go to his funeral. A young man brings her groceries. She hasn't been out of her house in forty years. She has that disease where she's afraid to go outside. But that's understandable in this town. A lot of senior citizens have it. Anyway, I once rented a room from her, so I know her pretty well. She's not a bad person, although she's addicted to black-and-white reruns on TV. I used to have to watch them every night, just to get to the news. While I lived there, we used to get all our water from her backyard well."

"But why do you think it's one of the wells Ms. Templeton was talking about?" Watch asked.

"Because I can't think of any other private well in town. Also, it's very deep. You have to lower your bucket way down to get any water. I used to get calluses on my hands trying to get a drink. The water you do get is ice cold. Remember how the witch mentioned the cold."

Watch scratched his head. "Is Ann Templeton really a witch? She seems so nice."

"Get on her bad side and you'll see how nice she is. I think the best way to understand her is to know that she does whatever amuses her. She has the power to do that. If it strikes her fancy, she'll save you from a thousand enemies. But if she's in a dark mood, she'll feed you to her boys."

"Who are her boys?" Watch asked

"You mean *what* are her boys. I don't want to talk about them tonight. We have enough problems." Bum pulled Watch down the street. "We have to hurry to

Mrs. Robinson's house. She does stay up late with her TV, but it's already two in the morning."

They reached the house twenty minutes later. It was an old wooden affair that stared out at the rock jetty and the burned-down lighthouse. Two stories tall, with a steeply pitched tar-paper roof, it didn't look as if it had been painted in the last two decades. Watch wondered how many other old people there were in Spooksville who never left their houses. Who just peered out from between their curtains and were terrified of the horrors that walked outside. Actually, Watch was amazed that anyone lived long enough in Spooksville to get old. He couldn't imagine he would last past his twenties. The thought didn't bother him, though. Not right now.

"You stay here on the sidewalk," Bum instructed. "It's better if I talk to her alone. She gets jittery around strangers. Last week a brand-new letter carrier tried to deliver her mail and she blew a hole in his mail bag with her shotgun."

"She has a shotgun?" Watch asked, amazed.

"Yeah, and she's a crack shot. Just give me a minute with her. She's proud of her well. If I tell her I have a friend who's just dying to taste the water from it, she'll let us run all over her backyard."

Bum was gone several minutes. Watch could see him

talking to someone on the front porch of the house, but with the shadows he couldn't tell who it was. When Bum returned, he was grinning.

"We can fool with her well all we want," Bum said. Watch noticed he had a flashlight in his hands and a coil of rope. The old woman must have given him the stuff. Bum didn't have a penny to his name, but whatever he needed just came to him. Watch wondered if Bum had powers of his own.

"I want to thank you for helping me rescue my friends," Watch said as they hurried around to the back of the house. Bum waved his hand.

"No problem," he said. "I like your friends."

"But you were ready to let them die when I first spoke to you."

Bum chuckled. "I was just hungry. When I haven't eaten in a couple of days, I never feel like rescuing anyone."

The well was nicely constructed. Built of gray bricks and a few white painted boards, it stood in the center of the backyard like a prized plant. It had a small roof over it, from which hung a rope, a pail, and a lowering winch. Watch wasn't sure what Bum had planned, but was sure it would be dangerous.

"You're not going to lower me down there, are

you?" Watch asked, when he saw Bum tying the extra rope onto one of the well's support poles. The question amused Bum.

"They're your friends," he said. "And better you than me."

Watch stared down into the black well. "How far down before I reach water?"

"At least two hundred feet."

"Can you lower me that far?"

"Lowering you is no problem. It's pulling you back up that'll be hard. I just hope my back doesn't give out."

Watch took Bum's flashlight and shone it down the well. Still, he couldn't see anything except pure blackness. But ever so faintly he did hear gurgling water. It sounded as if it was moving, an underground river.

"What if there's no room to breathe down there?" he asked. "To stand up?"

Bum nodded. "I thought of that. You might just end up in a cold pool, with no way out. If you do, shout for me to pull you back up."

Watch nodded as he swung a leg up onto the edge of the well. "Should I hang on to both the new rope and the old pail rope as I go down?" he asked.

"Yes," Bum said. "It'll decrease your chances that either of the ropes will break. You know, Watch, I have to admire your courage. If my friends were trapped down there, I wouldn't try to rescue them. Not that I have many friends."

"Does that mean if you can't pull me up, I'm doomed?"

"Exactly," Bum said cheerfully, slapping him on the back. "But I wish you the best of luck anyway."

Watch grabbed hold of both ropes. He kept the flashlight on and tucked it in his belt. He just hoped his glasses didn't fall off.

"Let's get this over with," he said.

Bum began to lower him down the deep shaft. Yet Watch didn't only depend on Bum's strength for support. The well was narrow. As he descended, he wedged himself against the opposite sides of the circular wall— his upper back jammed on one side, his feet on the other. Above, he could see Bum's face growing smaller and smaller. Soon it was just a dark dot against a black sky. Watch gripped the ropes tightly. He kept waiting for the feel of the water but it never came.

Yet the sound of the gurgling water grew louder. When Bum had become all but invisible, Watch felt a faint spray on his face. He stopped his descent and carefully pulled his flashlight from his belt. The well did not end in just water, but in a small air space. Panning around with the beam, he saw that two feet more and he would have burst free of the shaft, which now was dug out of bedrock. For the first time he hung with all his weight on the end of the two ropes and tried to peer around the edge of the shaft. What he needed to know was if there was only water below him. If there was no bedrock to lower himself on, he would have to abandon his rescue efforts.

And leave his friends to the Hyeets.

A moment later he saw that the well didn't draw its water from a pool. The black liquid twenty feet below him was definitely moving. If he wasn't messed up on his directions, it seemed to be flowing toward the ocean.

Watch found that interesting.

Unfortunately, as he stuck his head under the edge of the shaft, he could see no place to swim to. The underground river flowed out of one wall of blackness, and disappeared into another. It might reappear in an open space, but he couldn't drop down and take that chance. Swimming underwater and underground with the icy river, with nothing to breathe, he would drown in minutes.

A wave of sorrow swept over Watch then. It was rare that he allowed himself to experience any powerful emotion, but he had known Sally a long time. And in the last couple of weeks he had come to admire Adam a great deal. Plus Cindy was his friend as well. To lose all three of them at once would be horrible. He knew he needed to shout for Bum to pull him back up because there was nothing he could do. But Watch hesitated, straining to think of some way he could help his friends even if he couldn't see them.

But nothing came to Watch.

"Bum!" he shouted reluctantly. "Pull me up!"

The tension on both ropes increased. Bum was pulling with all his strength. Too bad he was the town bum instead of the physical education teacher. He wasn't that strong. Watch had to aid Bum's efforts by trying to crawl up the shaft, his upper back still jammed against one wall, his feet against the other. The problem was he was tired from the descent, and his strength was giving out, faster than he could have imagined. He tried to rest for brief moments by letting all his weight rest on the ropes, but Bum must have been tiring quickly also. When Watch did relax, he ended up slipping back down several feet.

This went on for over twenty minutes. At the end of that time, the top of the well was still far away. Watch wasn't sure what to do. He was breathing hard and his arms and legs and back ached terribly. He paused to take another quick break, to gather his strength. As he did so he let all his weight hang on the ropes.

Disaster struck quickly and without warning.

The ropes gave way and Watch fell.

There was nothing to do. He tried grasping at the walls of the shaft, but they slipped from his fingers. The overhead circle of sky shrank. Watch felt the cold air on his face just before the freezing water slapped his entire body.

Watch went under. He went down, into blackness.

He struggled frantically. Trying to reach a surface he couldn't see.

For a moment his head broke the surface.

He heard Bum shout from far overhead.

"I'm soooorrrryyyyyy!"

Then the current of the underground river gripped Watch and carried him against the far black wall and under the water once more. Where there was no light, and no air. He fought for a surface that didn't exist. The cold was crushing, his panic shattering. He was in a liquid tomb and there was absolutely no way out.

13

"WE HAVE TO SAVE HER," ADAM WAS SAY-
ing. "We can do it."

"How?" Sally asked. "Cindy had our only working
flashlight. It went when she went. We can't walk a hundred feet in this dark."

"What about the first flashlight? There was still a
little juice left in it."

"There's none now. I tried it a minute ago. The light's
dead."

"Let me see it," Adam demanded. They were standing just outside the volcanic chamber, on the exact spot
where Cindy had been swiped. Sally handed over the
flashlight, and Adam flipped the switch and pointed it

around the cave. He couldn't see a thing. "Why would it stop working?" he muttered.

"I may have accidentally turned it on while it was in my back pocket," Sally said. "It doesn't matter. It wouldn't have lasted five minutes."

Adam paced restlessly. "It does matter. We need only five minutes to save her."

"Adam—" Sally tried to speak.

He threw up his arms in frustration. "We were just sitting here talking and it took her. It moved so fast. I didn't even get a chance to grab her arm, to fight for her."

"You can't blame yourself," Sally said.

"Then who am I supposed to blame? I tell you, we have to go after her. We have to go now."

"But we won't be able to see where we're going," Sally protested.

"It doesn't matter. We can feel our way along the walls of the cave."

"That won't work for long. There're forks and side tunnels in this cave. We'll just end up lost in the dark."

"Then what do you think we should do?"

Sally hesitated. "Nothing."

Adam was exasperated. "We can't do anything! It'll kill her!"

Sally put her hand on his shoulder and spoke carefully.

"Adam, it's a big hairy monster. I know this isn't easy to hear, but it's probably already killed her. If we try to save Cindy, it will just kill us."

Adam was angry. "You just don't like her. You're jealous of her. You don't care if it eats her. In fact, you're probably happy it grabbed her."

Sally spoke patiently. "Earlier tonight I risked my life to save Cindy. I'm sure you haven't forgotten. Yeah, sure, I yell at her every five minutes. But that doesn't mean I don't like her. I yell at you all the time. If I thought there was a chance we could rescue her, I'd take that chance. But there's no hope. We don't even know where it took her."

Adam pointed down the cave, in the direction they hadn't gone yet. "They went that way. I'm going that way. I don't care what you say."

"You'll lose your way in a few minutes," Sally said.

Adam looked down at his pile of boards. "Maybe not. Dipped in lava, these boards could work as torches. If we get them burning bright enough, we might even be able to use them as weapons. Most animals are afraid of fire. I bet this creature is, too."

Sally considered the idea. "The wood won't burn for long."

"It may not have taken her far." Adam paused and added reluctantly, "If it's that hungry."

Sally glanced into the volcanic chamber, then nodded wearily. "If you want to try, I'll go with you. There's no use in staying here anyway. I'm never going to get that magic door to open. If it is a door."

They gathered together their boards. Approaching the boiling pools, they had no trouble soaking the tips of the boards with molten lava. Tiny flames flared around the edges of the lava lumps, but the sticks didn't burst into flames, which was good. The torches didn't give off much light, but it appeared they'd last longer than a few minutes. They made only two torches. They figured they could always light the other sticks and transfer the lava when the first boards had burned down.

They set off at a brisk walk. They were fortunate the creature had left huge tracks in the dirt floor, because they soon came to another fork in the tunnel. The thing had gone to the right so they went to the right. Based on its foot size, Adam figured the creature must be eight feet tall. In the dismal red glow of their torches, he searched for signs of Cindy's blood on the cave floor. He prayed the whole time. If he saw her blood, he knew he would lose all hope.

They reached another fork. This time the creature had veered to the left. Making the turn, they felt a sudden drop in temperature. The change was remarkable.

But they were soon given a reason for the coolness. Ten minutes along this new path and they came to a cold black river. This last portion of cave had widened considerably. The river flowed along the right side, hugging the wall. They were desperate to save their friend, but they both took a moment to fall to their knees to take a drink. Adam swallowed so much cold water so quickly his tongue momentarily froze and he had trouble speaking. Sally gulped away beside him.

"I never thought water could taste so good," she mumbled. "This is better than my morning coffee."

Adam grunted. "Good. Hmm."

"I wonder where this river leads?"

Adam looked around. It led in the direction the creature had taken Cindy. He climbed back to his feet, anxious to resume the hunt. He grabbed his dull red torch and worked his tongue in his mouth.

"We'll see," he said. "Let's go."

But then Sally suddenly grabbed his arm.

"Adam!" she screamed, pointing. "A horrible fish monster is coming out of the river! Look!"

Adam turned to see a big white object struggling in the stream. It seemed to have emerged from just under the far wall. Since their torches gave off as much light as a fat cigar, neither of them could make out its shape right away. But it seemed—Adam stopped and rubbed his eyes—to be wearing glasses.

"Watch?" Adam gasped. "Is that you?"

The terrible monster grabbed the bank of the river and peered up at them through thick lenses. It was gasping for breath and shivering uncontrollably.

"Yeah, it's me," he whispered. "Is that you, Adam?"

"Yeah. Sally and I are both here. I'll give you a hand." They pulled Watch from the water. He was as cold as a Popsicle. He couldn't even stand at first, he was so numb. He lay on the floor of the cave, trying to catch his breath and wiping the water off his glasses.

"I'm glad these didn't fall off," he said. "Can't see a thing without them."

Adam and Sally knelt by his side. They tried rubbing his arms and legs to restore his circulation. His shivering began to lessen.

"But where did you come from?" Adam asked.

Watch sat up with effort. "Mrs. Robinson's backyard," he said.

"Who's Mrs. Robinson?" Adam asked.

Sally made a face. "I know her. She's a creepy old woman who never leaves her house. Ten years ago she poisoned her husband and didn't even have the decency to attend his funeral."

"I don't know about that," Watch said. "But she's got a deep well in the middle of her backyard." Watch went on to give them a brief explanation of what he had done since they last saw him. He even related what the witch had said. Adam found it all very fascinating, but he was still anxious to go after Cindy. He helped Watch to his feet.

"How long were you underwater?" Adam asked.

Watch coughed. "Just a couple of minutes. But it was a long two minutes."

Adam noticed he was carrying a flashlight. "Does your light work?"

Watch tried it. Nothing. "I guess the water got to the batteries."

"You wouldn't happen to have a high-powered pistol in your pocket?" Sally asked.

"No." Watch blinked. "Where's Cindy?"

"An ape creature grabbed her," Adam explained. "It's been about twenty minutes since she disappeared." He pointed to the floor. "We're following these tracks. Are you strong enough to walk?"

Watch nodded. "I think it would warm me up. But I have to warn you guys about these creatures. They're called Hyeets and they're supposed to take no prisoners."

"Then we'd better hurry," Adam said. "Come on."

14

THE CAVE FORKED ANOTHER THREE TIMES, but the footprints remained clear. Fifteen minutes after finding Watch, Adam heard sounds up ahead. He raised his hand, cautioning the others to slow their pace. He could hear a faint growling—that was clear enough. But he also thought he heard Cindy's voice.

"What's going on here?" he whispered aloud.

"Maybe they're saying grace together before dinner," Sally suggested. "Maybe Cindy doesn't realize she is the main course."

"I have water in my ears," Watch apologized. "I can't hear anything."

"Maybe you two should wait here," Adam said. "There's no sense in all of us being killed."

"Nonsense," Sally said. "If we have to fight the monster, we'll fight it together. That way we might stand a chance."

Adam agreed with her logic. They crept forward cautiously. Another hundred feet and it was clear both Cindy and the Hyeet were making noise. The weird thing was, Cindy didn't act hysterical.

They reached another turn. Adam made them stop.

Cindy and the Hyeet appeared to be just around the corner.

"This is it," Adam whispered. "We fight to the death."

"We don't take prisoners either," Sally agreed.

"I can't believe I let myself get mixed up in this," Watch remarked.

They raised their torches and ran around the corner.

They stopped dead in their tracks.

Cindy looked over at them. "Hi, guys. Glad you could make it."

The Hyeet, the loathsome evil monster, was indeed eight feet tall. Clearly it was a cross between a man and an ape—the fabled missing link. Except for around its eyes, nose, and mouth, it was covered with black hair. Its nose was wide; the nostrils flared as it drew in hungry breaths. It had massive hands, large feet. But it was its eyes that were the most peculiar. They were bigger than those of a human, but were an eerie green. They seemed to glow in the dark. Whirling at the sudden intrusion of three small humans, it looked as if its eyes might burst from its head. It scampered backward and hugged its midsection with its hands. Cindy had been sitting down with her back to a wall, but she jumped to her feet and held up her own hands.

"Don't scare it," she pleaded.

"Don't scare it?" Sally asked. "We're here to kill it."

Cindy shook her head. "No. We had it all wrong. This creature means us no harm. In fact, I think it's more afraid of us than we are of it."

"If that's true," Adam said—although he was relieved to see Cindy all in one piece—"why did it grab you and carry you off?"

He asked the question angrily because he couldn't help noticing that their only working flashlight lay broken on the ground. Perhaps it had fallen from her hands while she was being carried by the creature. Perhaps the light had scared the creature, and it had broken it deliberately. It didn't really matter, the flashlight wasn't going to work anymore. The batteries themselves appeared damaged.

"Because it's desperate," Cindy said. "I think it needs our help."

"Our help with what?" Sally asked. "Preparing vampire bats for dinner?"

Cindy glanced at the creature, which continued to hug the far wall. Adam noticed that it was trembling. It may even have been weeping, its green eyes were moist. It was no longer growling, now it was whimpering. And it looked to Cindy to defend it, even though it was five times her size.

"I don't know what it needs," Cindy said. "It's been trying to communicate with me using sign language."

Sally frowned "Is it deaf?"

Cindy was annoyed. "No. But it doesn't speak English."

"Well, if it wants to live in Spooksville it should learn," Sally said.

Adam lowered his torch. He'd had experience talking to strange creatures. Why, the previous week he had talked down a ghost from an astral rage. He thought he might be able to handle the Hyeet. As he took a step toward it, it pushed itself against the wall.

"We won't hurt you," he said in a gentle voice. "We want to help you. We want you to help us. What is it you need?" Adam pointed at it and smiled. "You," he said again.

The Hyeet seemed to relax slightly. It gestured to them with one of its hairy paws. "Rrrrlllloooo," it said.

Sally glanced at Watch. "Did the witch teach you what that meant?"

"She only taught me two words in Reeksvar," Watch replied. "One for *open*, the other for *close*."

"Reeksvars," Adam said to the creature, nodding his head "Reeksvars?"

The creature nodded "Reekssss," it said.

"I think we're making progress," Adam remarked.

"You could have fooled me," Sally said. "Find out what the beast wants and ask it the way out of here. Then I'll be impressed."

"I have received the impression this creature is alone here in these caves," Cindy said. "The way it hugs itself, and shakes back and forth, it's like it has lost all its friends and family. Once it started communicating with me, it got all excited."

"You could tell all that by its gestures?" Adam asked, impressed.

Cindy shook her head. "I think it can understand more of what we're saying than we can understand of what it's saying." She paused. "I wonder if it can read our minds. Not clearly, I mean, but that it can pick up on the sense of what we're saying."

"It might simply be smarter than we are," Watch said.

"Speak for yourself," Sally said.

"If it has lost its friends," Adam said. "We have to ask ourselves where it lost them?"

"The bats might have got them," Cindy suggested.

"I don't think so," Adam said. "Bats and spiders probably don't bother the Hyeet one bit. It is used to living underground." He glanced at Sally. "Do you have any theories on where the other Hyeets might have gone?"

Realization dawned on Sally. "Through the mysterious doorway!" she exclaimed. Then she paused. "Wait a second. Why would this one have been left behind? And even if it was left behind, why would it be unable to open the door by itself?"

"There could be a thousand answers to those questions," Adam said. "But it's curious Ms. Templeton taught Watch the two words that she did. You say she's a witch. I don't know if that's true. But I do know she's got power. Last time I ran into her, she told me something that was going to happen later in the day. And it did happen—I met Bum and passed through the Secret Path. She might be able to see into the future. She might have given Watch those two words because they can be used to control the mysterious doorway."

"It might have been the Reeksvars who cut this doorway into the wall you're talking about," Watch suggested.

"You haven't even seen it," Sally protested.

Watch shrugged. "I'd like to—if it leads out of this place."

"You only just got here," Sally said. "Try being here all night."

"Try watching Bum eat an eight-course meal," Watch replied.

"But even if these special words open the doorway," Sally said. "There's no guarantee that it will lead us back to the surface. From the sound of things, it probably just leads to more Hyeets. I mean no offense, but this guy needs a bath. If I have to live with a whole herd of them for the rest of my life, I will go mental."

Adam nodded. "It's possible we'll help this creature and still be trapped here. But we have to give it a try. Besides, we don't have anything else we can do right now to help ourselves."

Adam turned to the Hyeet and pointed back in the direction of the volcanic chamber. Then he gestured to the lava at the tip of his torch. The creature could very well have been telepathic. The Hyeet seemed to understand. It nodded vigorously. It wanted them to return to that place with it. To Adam's amazement, it offered Adam its big hairy hand.

"I think you've made a friend," Sally said sweetly.

Adam took the Hyeet's hand and looked up into its weird green eyes. They were like large phosphorescent marbles. Adam had to smile; the creature appeared anxious for them to like it. The Hyeet tried to grin, but the expression ended up resembling something an ape would do while stuffing its face with bananas. The Hyeet accidentally drooled on Adam's arm. Afraid to offend it, Adam didn't immediately wipe off the mess.

"You never know who you're going to meet when you wake up in the morning," Adam said.

15

THE STRANGE RECTANGULAR SHAPE STOOD etched in the black wall before them. Only twenty feet at their backs, the lava pools bubbled and hissed. The Hyeet stared at the shape with something like reverence, mixed with sorrow. Clearly the creature had come here many times in the past and gazed hungrily at the markings on the wall. Adam worried that if the special words Watch had brought from Ann Templeton failed, the Hyeet would have a nervous breakdown. It continued to look at them with such hope. Adam had to take his hand back. The Hyeet seemed afraid to let go of him. Adam coughed and cleared his throat. The fumes were as bad as before. Watch had already told Adam of *Bela*—open—and *Nela*—close.

"We don't know what will happen when we say these words," Adam said. "The rest of you should stand back."

Sally reluctantly agreed. "Just don't let yourself get sucked into a prehistoric zoo," she warned.

A moment later Adam was left alone with the Hyeet before what they hoped was a secret doorway. The others bunched together at the entrance to the chamber. Adam turned and patted the Hyeet on the back. Again the creature tried to smile. It shouldn't have bothered; it just ended up drooling more on Adam.

"Don't eat me if this doesn't work," Adam said.

The Hyeet's eyes moistened again.

It would never do such a thing it seemed to want to say.

Adam turned back to the etchings and took a deep breath.

"*Bela!*" he shouted.

Nothing happened. For three seconds.

Then many things happened at once.

The wall inside the deeply carved lines began to glow. It took on a blue radiance. The bright color was at complete odds with the sober red of the volcanic pit. The light quickly grew in intensity. Adam had to shield his eyes with his hand. But peeking between his fingers, he saw that not only was the wall glowing, it was becoming transparent. It was as if the black stone was turning to clear glass.

The window began to open.

The scenery that lay beyond was staggering.

Adam glimpsed endless rolling green fields, jungles with trees as tall as mountains, lakes where turtles as large as bears swam. The sky was a brilliant blue. The sun that shone in it seemed twice as big as normal, ten times as bright. Adam briefly wondered if he was looking at the world as it had appeared millions of years ago. Or maybe the doorway opened into another dimension or into another solar system.

Far in the distance he could see other Hyeets.

The Hyeet beside him saw them, too.

The creature squealed with joy and slapped Adam on the back.

Adam almost fell through the magical doorway.

"You go ahead." He gasped, catching the edge of the portal. "Say hi to your friends for me. Enjoy a good meal. I'm sure after eating all those bats, you could use one."

The Hyeet tried to smile one last time. This third effort was as miserable as the first two. But then the creature did the most incredible thing. It put its hand over Adam's heart and worked its wide mouth into a semblance of a human form.

"Adam," it said with feeling.

Adam had to laugh. "Wow."

Then the Hyeet leaped forward, toward the now transparent wall, and was gone. Adam blinked; the Hyeet simply vanished. But Adam thought he caught a glimpse of it running across the wide grass field, yelping in joy, although he wasn't sure. At the moment Adam had other things to worry about.

A strong air suction had started in front of the portal. It was as if a huge fan had been turned on in the other land, and set backward before the doorway. Adam had to hold on to the edge tightly to keep from being sucked in. Behind him, the lava pools hissed. The force of the suction was disturbing the sleeping fires. Adam realized he was on the verge of starting a minor eruption. And he knew he had only to say the word and the doorway would close and everything would return to normal. But for some reason—perhaps it was because he was hanging on for dear life—he couldn't remember what the Reeksvar word for *close* was.

"*Bela!*" he shouted into the howling wind. "Rela! Stela! Mela! Kela! Tela!"

No, none of those were right. Adam feared he was never going to get it. Raising his right leg, he pressed his foot against the side of the doorway and pushed back as hard as he could. He landed on his butt, but was immediately shaken by the suction force. He didn't give it a chance to pull on him again. Reaching out, he grasped the edge of a large black boulder and pulled himself farther away from the howling wind. He did the same with a series of rocks. The lava pools were furious now. Steam gushed toward the ceiling, just about wiping out all visibility. Adam felt the ground shake as he labored to climb to his feet. Something was on the verge of blowing.

Adam made it back to where his friends were waiting.

"What happened?" Sally demanded.

"The Hyeet escaped back to his home," Adam said.

"We saw that," Cindy said. "But why didn't you close the door?"

"Did you shout out the word?" Watch asked.

Adam glanced at the collapsing chamber. "What was the word again?" he asked rather sheepishly.

"*Nela!*" all three of them said at once.

Adam grimaced. "I was close. I should have kept trying."

"Well, you can't try now," Sally said, pointing to what was happening only a few feet from where they stood. There was so much steam, dust, and exploding lava, the magical doorway was completely invisible. Sally shouted over the noise, "We have to get out of here!"

They ran back in the direction of the cold river. It didn't take many turns of the cave to bring them out of the range of the eruption. Soon it was dark again, silent and gloomy. They had saved the Hyeet, but they still didn't know how to save themselves. Worst of all, their meager torches were ready to go out, and they had left their few remaining boards back in the volcanic chamber. They stumbled in the seemingly endless night beside the icy water. Adam had reached the point where he was willing to try anything.

"What if we swim underground?" he asked Watch. "Back the way you came? We might be able to reach the spot where the well comes down. Bum might still be there and be able to help us out."

Watch shook his head. "That's impossible. None of us would be able to swim against the current. I almost drowned, and I was flowing with it. Also, we would never get up the well. It's too hard."

"It's a chance," Cindy said.

"Believe me, it's no chance at all," Watch said. "We have to find another way out."

Sally pointed anxiously at their two waning torches. "We only have a few minutes left. There's no other way out."

But just then Adam had an incredible idea.

336

It was the best idea he'd had all night.

"Watch," he said. "When you came down the well, could you tell which direction the river beneath you was flowing?"

Watch didn't hesitate. "It was headed toward the ocean. I thought of that. But we all already know there's no cave opening down by the beach."

"And the water is full of sharks," Sally said.

"None of that matters," Adam said. "I have a plan. We're going to keep following this river."

"What if our lights fail?" Sally demanded. "What if we run into a dead end?"

Adam repeated himself, but with an odd confidence in his voice. "None of that matters."

The river rushed forward. They chased it, running now. But they could not run far because the inevitable finally caught up with them. The remaining lumps of lava wrapped around their boards gasped and died. The faint red glow went out. It had been a miserable light, but any light was welcome when darkness was all around. They missed it dearly. They dropped the torches in the black river, but couldn't see as the current carried them away. Their mad dash was finished. They would have to move slowly now, led only by the sound of the water, the touch of their fingers. Adam told them not to lose hope. Someone clasped his hand. He assumed it was Cindy, but it was Sally.

"Did you know I sleep with a night-light on?" she said softly.

"You?" he asked in the perfect dark. "I don't believe it."

Her fingers squeezed his tight. "I've always been afraid of the dark."

"I'm afraid of it now," Cindy whispered from somewhere close.

"I know what I'm doing," Adam said, hoping that he did.

The others had their doubts thirty minutes later.

They ran into a dead end.

The cave just stopped at a stone wall.

The river disappeared under the ground.

End of the road. Nowhere left to go.

Adam heard the sounds of his friends despair all around him. He spoke in what he hoped was an upbeat voice. "Watch," he said. "What time is it?"

Adam knew all of Watch's watches had phosphorescent hands.

"Six-ten in the morning," Watch said. "Why?"

Adam sat down on the ground beside the river, telling the others to do the same. "We're going to wait," he said.

"For what?" Sally asked. "To die?"

"No," he said. "To be rescued."

"No one will come to rescue us," Cindy said sadly.

"I didn't say it would be a person," Adam replied. "Be patient. You'll see."

Several minutes went by while they listened to their breathing. Perhaps they also listened to their own heartbeats.

"I'm getting cold," Sally said finally.

"You'll be warm soon," Adam promised. "A few more minutes."

More minutes crawled by.

Sally started to speak again. But her voice caught in her throat.

Something magical was happening. The water beside them began to glow. It grew in brightness quickly. Soon they were able to see each other again. Adam had to laugh at their astounded faces.

"Is it another magic portal?" Cindy asked.

Adam laughed. "No, it's not magic. Watch, what time is it now?"

Watch checked his timepieces. "Six thirty-six."

Sally gasped. "That's when the sun comes up! We're seeing the light of dawn!"

Adam stood. "Yes. That's it. This stream runs into the

ocean. For us to see the sunlight at all, we must be close to the outside. I bet we only have to swim the length of a backyard pool underwater and we'll be out in the fresh air."

"But how can you know for sure the ocean is right out there?" Cindy asked.

"Taste the water," Adam said.

All three of his friends tried it. "It tastes slightly salty," Cindy said.

"Naturally," Adam said. "Here where the river and the ocean meet, some of the saltwater must push upstream."

"But you got the idea to come here a mile back," Sally insisted. "How could you be sure we'd find the sun?"

Adam laughed again. "I was hoping we'd find it. But all rivers run to the sea, as the old saying goes. Why should this one be different?" He tore off his filthy shirt and kicked off his dirty shoes. "I'm going first. If I'm not back in a minute or two, I don't know what to tell you guys. I've probably gone for milk and doughnuts."

Adam dived in before they could respond.

He was back a minute later, grinning from ear to ear.

"This river comes out right near the jetty," he said. "We're not far from the burned-down lighthouse."

"Oh, no." Cindy groaned. "I hope the ghost is still gone."

"The ghost?" Sally asked. "Who cares about a ghost?"

She stood and began to walk back into the cave. "I'm still worried about that shark we saw last week. There's no way I'm going out this way. I'm hiking back to the reservoir. I don't care if it takes me till next week."

They tried to convince Sally it was a lousy idea, but she was stubborn and wouldn't listen. In the end they had to drag her, kicking and screaming, underwater, and then out onto the jetty. But once she was standing in the fresh air, she quickly forgave them. It looked like it was going to be another sunny day. Sally smiled brightly.

"Who wants ice cream?" she asked. "You can have any flavor you want."

Adam smiled. "As long as it's vanilla?"

Sally pinched his cheek. "That's true. But today, Adam, I feel like treating."

Molly Bigelow is NOT your average girl. She's one of an elite
crew assigned the task of policing and protecting the zombie
population of New York. *The Hunger Games* author
Suzanne Collins says *Dead City* "breathes new life
into the zombie genre."

EBOOK EDITIONS
ALSO AVAILABLE

Adventure awaits in the Five Kingdoms—

by the *New York Times* bestselling author Brandon Mull.

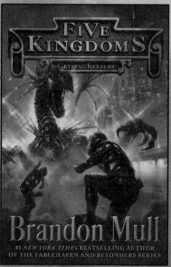